As a coroner, medusa Seremela Telemar has always felt more comfortable chatting over a dead body than over drinks. But when her wild niece, Vetta, runs off to Devil's Gate, a lawless town that sprung up overnight in a modern-day gold rush, she knows she has to extricate her before the rebellious girl gets into real trouble.

Vampyre Duncan Turner is not about to let his new co-worker go into that chaotic Wild West town alone. His Vampyric power and lawyer smarts make him the perfect ally, and the fact that he already had his eye on Seremela for more…personal reasons, doesn't hurt matters. Any romantic thoughts are put on hold, however, when they arrive at Devil's Gate and learn Vetta is set to hang by morning.

In order to save Vetta and themselves, Seremela and Duncan are going to have to fight fire with force, and magic with fangs. And pray they make it out of Devil's Gate alive.

δevil's Gate

Thea Harrison

Devil's Gate
Copyright © 2012 by Teddy Harrison LLC
ISBN 13: 978-1-947046-98-6
Print Edition

Cover Photo-illustration © Kanaxa

This title was previously published and is being rereleased by the author. It has not been revised.

Chapter One

Sacrifice

SEREMELA TELEMAR LEANED against the frame of the open balcony doors in her high-rise apartment and looked out at the ocean view. Tropical humidity licked her skin. As soon as she had gotten home, she had opened up the balcony doors, stripped off her work clothes and put on denim shorts and a tank top.

The weather in Miami was playing the blues. Like the singer Nina Simone's voice, it had a dark, sultry vibe with a bitter edge and an unexpected snap. Massive knots of moody clouds obscured the sun as they roiled over turbulent water, and heavy rain lashed down in vertical sheets. All that was needed was a world-weary man in a Bogart suit, fingering ivory piano keys in an abandoned hotel as he waited for a hurricane.

One of her head snakes slipped over her shoulder and rose to look at her, its jeweled gaze curious. It tasted the storm-laden air with a slender tongue. She put a forefinger underneath its jaw and nudged it gently. It slid closer and rested its tiny cheek against hers. In another mood, she might have smiled, but not this morning.

Was she really going to do this again?

Yes. Yes, she was.

She sighed, turned on her cell phone and hit speed dial. She held it up to her ear. A strained feminine voice on the other end said, "Serrie?"

"Yes," she said to her sister, Camilla. "I'll go get her."

"Oh, thank the gods," Camilla said fervently.

"I do not believe the gods are whom you should be thanking," said Seremela.

"Of course not!" Camilla said. "Thank you, Serrie! You know how much this means to me. Vetta won't mind me at all anymore—she never listens to anything I say, and I know what would happen if I tried to fetch her home myself. It would blow up into everything being my fault again, and the fight would drag on for hours and hours—and Vetta would make it as public as she could just to humiliate me, she knows how much I hate public altercations—"

"Camilla," Seremela said. Her tone was sharp enough that it cut through Camilla's babble. The other woman fell silent. She said, "I need for you to listen to me right now."

"Of course, whatever you need," Camilla said quickly.

"This is the last time I'm going to be able to drop everything to help fix your problems and your mistakes."

Camilla's tone turned cautious. "What do you mean,

the last time?"

"I can't keep putting my life on hold every time something goes wrong for you, or every time you and Vetta have an argument that you can't resolve. I just started a new, very demanding job. My employers are wonderful people, and they're really good to me, but there's only so much I can ask from them. Unlimited time off at a moment's notice is not one of those things."

Camilla's voice turned cold. "She's your niece. I thought you cared about what happened to her."

Seremela bit back her anger. Now it was time for the guilt trip, but it was always time for the guilt trip whenever she didn't do what Camilla wanted her to do, or say what Camilla wanted to hear. Children were rare for all of the Elder Races, and ever since Camilla had managed to carry Vetta to term, she had a skewed perspective on what the world owed her for achieving such a precious miracle.

"Of course I love both of you," she said. "And I care about what happens to you. That's why I'm agreeing to make this trip. But she's your daughter, and I have to agree, Vetta's out of control. You have to figure out how to work things out with her yourself. You need to get counseling, Camilla, not only for yourself but for Vetta too."

"I have to go," Camilla said.

Seremela rolled her eyes. "Sure you do," she said. She spoke too late, and a dial tone sounded in her ear.

Camilla had hung up on her.

She resisted the urge to throw her iPhone. Instead she checked her work email again. Still no response from either of her new employers, Carling or Rune.

To be fair, she had only emailed them a short while ago, when she had gone into the office to ready her desk for a leave of absence. Deep regrets, family emergency, need to take time off work, will be in touch soon, blah blah blah. She had written the same kind of letter so often through the years, she could compose one in her sleep.

How many times had she sacrificed herself on the altar of Camilla's neediness? She blew out a breath. Too many times to count.

If she expected Camilla to learn to take responsibility for her own life, Seremela had to do the same. She had chosen to enable Camilla's behavior over the years. Now it was time to focus her energy on building a new life for herself.

After all, that's what her move to Miami was all about: taking on a new job and doing medical research she really wanted to do, building a new life and exploring new opportunities and horizons. It was not too late for her to break out of her sheltered, academic shell.

The small, poisonous voice of her Adversary whispered, the only confidence you ever found was in the classroom or the laboratory. When you're not lecturing over an autopsied body, you turn into a klutzy fool. You haven't dated in years—actually decades now—and you rarely make new friends. You're never going to have children of your own, and you've grown set in your ways as well. You're starting a new life with the old you. All your old problems and old weaknesses have come with you, so how can you expect to truly change anything?

She rubbed her forehead tiredly. The medusae believed that each medusa was born with a drop of poison in their souls. The poison turned into the medusa's Adversary, the dark voice that whispered doubts and fears in one's own thoughts. The measure of one's strength was determined by how well one withstood one's internal Adversary. Seremela tried to overcome that negative voice, but her own Adversary had a lot of ammunition to use against her.

She forced herself to concentrate on the task at hand. There was no reason to procrastinate any longer by pretending that she was waiting to hear back from her bosses. Many employers were very understanding about family emergencies—at least the first time. And Carling and Rune were much better than many other employers. They had gone out of their way to show her how much they valued her.

She sighed, tossed her phone onto the coffee table and went to pack a carry-on. Seriously, when she found Vetta, she was going to wring that girl's neck. That'd solve any potential problems with further confrontation or conflict. It wouldn't cure Camilla of her neediness or get Seremela a life outside of work, but that was okay, it would make room for taking care of the rest. Lots and lots of lovely room.

A knock sounded on her apartment door. The nictating membrane on her eyes snapped shut in surprise, and she paused, bras clutched in one hand and undies in the other. Dropping the filmy, colorful handfuls of underwear into her open case, she hurried to the door and peered out the peephole.

A dark haired man stood on the other side of her door, looking like he had just stepped out of an issue of GQ magazine. He stood in a casual stance, hands in the pockets of a hand-stitched linen summer suit, the jacket unbuttoned. Every expensive line of the tailored clothes emphasized his lean, well shaped body. His sleek dark hair, layered in a razor cut, fell on his forehead as though he had just run his fingers through it. His eyes were just as dark as his hair and glittered with intelligence. In contrast his skin was the pale ivory of a man who never saw any sunlight.

Because if he did, he would vanish in a blaze of fire.

Duncan Turner, internationally famous lawyer and the youngest progeny of one of the most Powerful Vampyres in the world, stood on her doorstep? In midmorning?

Once her nictating membranes started they wouldn't stop. They snapped open. Shut again. Open again. Shut again. It was a medusa's version of nervous hiccups.

She jerked her head back and rubbed at her eyes quickly to make them stop. When she opened her eyes again, she saw that several of her snakes were trying to look through the peephole, pushing each other out of the way.

She grabbed at her snakes, gathering them up frantically. They kept sliding out of her hands, trying to get back to the peephole.

Forget about dating. This is why I don't play poker, she thought. *Because I have so many tells, and they're all so opinionated.*

Duncan knocked on the door again, making her jump. "Seremela?" he called. "Are you home?"

Even through the door, his rich, baritone voice sent shivers down her skin. Her agitation sent all her snakes undulating.

For crying out loud, stop it! she told them telepathically. Out loud, she said, "Yes, I—I'm home! Hold on just a moment. I'll be right with you!"

Now all of her snakes were trying to look out the door. They knew Duncan was outside too. They liked Duncan. A lot.

"Calm down, damn it," she hissed out loud.

As usual, they ignored her. Some elderly medusae were famous for their control over their head snakes, and everything they did or said was a graceful symphony of coordinated movement.

Not Seremela. Oh no, hers never paid attention to a word she said to them, and she had long since given up hope of exerting any true control over them. They were like a pack of poorly trained poodles.

"Seremela?" Duncan said.

He sounded…complex, but then he always sounded complex, the flavors and notes in his voice as layered as a fine, aged wine. He was a master of nuance and one of the sharpest legal minds in the world, and—and she admired him so damn much, it tied her up in knots.

And it didn't help in the slightest that his voice, like actors Alan Rickman or Liam Neeson, was spellbindingly beautiful. According to Carling, Duncan rarely made court appearances any longer, but when he did, other lawyers, judges and legal professionals from different demesnes traveled from all over the world just to hear him speak.

Now he sounded divided between amusement and worry.

"Everything's all right," she called out as she patted the door. That was a stupid thing to say, especially in the face of her family emergency. If she could, she would climb in bed and pull the covers over her head. Over all their heads. "You just caught me by surprise. Hold on a moment."

"Take your time," he said.

His voice. Swear to gods, she was pretty sure he could bring her to orgasm just by talking.

That thought did nothing to help her present a cool, collected attitude of her own, nor did it help to calm down her excited little head freaks. She threw up her hands and dashed across the apartment, back to her bedroom where she grabbed a scarf and wound it around the snakes with quick expertise, starting at the back of her head.

The normal life span for medusae was around 450-500 years, and their snakes grew longer and more poisonous as they aged. Infants and small children had snakes as small as their fingers, the poison from their bites about as irritating as a mosquito bite, while elders had snakes that often trailed a foot or so along the ground. A single bite from the snake of an elder could make a grown human very sick, and multiple bites would cause almost certain death to several races.

Seremela was in late middle age, close to 380 years old, and her snakes reached past her hips. She had never felt threatened or afraid enough to cause her snakes to bite anyone. She pulled the mass over one shoulder and worked quickly down their length.

They did not want to be wrapped in the scarf—really, it was like putting children down for a nap—and their agitation increased until she had them all snugly under cover and eased them back over her shoulder again. Once they were tucked in a warm, dark place, they went quiet. Even as she stepped out of the bedroom, she could sense that they were asleep.

She took a deep breath and hurried back to open the door. Duncan, who stood looking down the hall as he waited, turned back quickly to face her. His dark, clever gaze regarded her for a moment. She felt her cheeks grow warm at the open concern in his expression.

She held the door open wider, more to give herself

an excuse to back away from his penetrating, too observant attention than to be hospitable, although she did manage to say, "Please, do come in."

"Thank you." Hands still tucked in his pockets, Duncan strolled into her apartment.

Her mouth dried as she watched him. In some ways he looked so normal. At five foot ten or so, he stood just a few inches taller than she did. And he wasn't oversized. He had a neat, compact build, and when he moved something unique and intangible became manifest, as his sharp, quiet intelligence flowed through his body.

All Vampyres had the same liquid, inhuman grace, but not all of them affected Seremela the same way that Duncan did. She ducked her head and shut the door. When she turned around to face him, she found him studying her again. She grew even more self-conscious, too aware of the amount of bare skin exposed by the skimpy, thin material of her red tank top and her shorts. Her toenails were painted a bright, saucy lime green. She glanced down at her bare legs then back up at him.

If only she had her work clothes on, and a dissected corpse on a table between them. Then she would know what to say and how to act.

Still, she had to start somewhere. She said, "I wasn't expecting company."

"I hope you don't mind that I stopped by unannounced," he said.

His voice moved over her in an invisible caress. She shivered as her mind supplied her with images garnered from her earlier storm-washed fancy: Duncan, dressed in a Bogart suit, stroking long, clever fingers on piano keys, with his dark head bent and a melancholy gaze. Then she steps into the room and he turns to her with fierce joy— giving her a look that says they are the only two people in the world—

Heavy reality thudded into place around her. Gah. Where were they? Oh, he had said something. That meant it was her turn, right? Argh, where was a dead body when you needed one the most? She fumbled for an appropriate response. "No, of course not."

His gaze had lingered at her head. He gave her a small, grave smile. "I'm sorry to see the little rascals are tucked away today."

Warmed, she touched the back of her head with a self-conscious hand. Many people were afraid or repulsed by a medusa's snakes, and at various times throughout history, medusae had been persecuted and killed because of it. The most famous example of a medusa being murdered was in ancient Greece, when Perseus had beheaded a woman who was supposedly so ugly, the sight of her could turn people into stone.

But Duncan wasn't like most other people. He seemed to enjoy the snakes, and he had treated them with indulgent amusement when they had flirted with him at Carling and Rune's winter solstice Masque party.

Her snakes didn't have the slightest problem with social situations—not that they ever behaved appropriately.

Once at a work party, she grew lightheaded and extremely giddy while she talked with the woman who was her boss at that time. When she turned around, she caught several of her snakes lapping at leftover alcohol in the bottom of several glasses on a table behind her. Thankfully her boss had been amused and helped to call her a cab ride home.

"They needed a time out," she confessed. "What a surprise to see you, Duncan, especially in the middle of the day."

His smile widened briefly before it disappeared. He said, "I remembered the layout of your apartment building and the basement garage from when I dropped you off after the Masque party. It's a simple matter to park in the garage and come up the elevator, and the windows at the end of the hallway are quite easy to avoid. This building is very Vampyre friendly."

"I see," she said.

Duncan drove a silver Aston Martin V12 Zagato with windows that had been tinted with full spectrum UV protection. The price tag on the car had to be well in excess of half a million dollars, but when you were the founding partner of one of the premiere law firms in the United States that specialized in Elder Races inter demesne law, you could afford some unusually nice perks.

She glanced at the open balcony doors that led out to a wide patio. Not only did she and Duncan stand well away from them, but it was still dark outside and raining hard. Even though her apartment faced the east, there wasn't any danger of sunshine streaming in the windows until the storm blew away.

No doubt Duncan had already calculated all of that even as he stepped inside her apartment. For him, any contact with the sun would be excruciating and would turn lethal within a matter of seconds. He must be aware of the sun's position every moment of his life.

She turned back to him and met his gaze. "What can I do for you?"

"I'm butting in where I haven't been invited, Seremela," he said bluntly. "And I hope you forgive me for it. I happened to be in a meeting with Carling when she received your email. I know you have a family emergency, and I wanted to stop by to make sure you were okay."

Her lips parted and her eyes widened. She had left her medical examiner position in Illinois and moved to Miami to focus on private medical research for Carling and Rune. Ever since then she had enjoyed getting to know Duncan.

Duncan was Carling's youngest progeny, and as Carling and Rune's lawyer, he was working closely with them on setting up their new agency. Seremela was one of the agency's first employees.

Duncan wasn't Seremela's boss, by any means, but he would be aware of any administrative decisions Carling and Rune made, and they certainly wouldn't hesitate to mention confidential matters to him.

As their group was small and most were new to the area, they tended to socialize together as well as work together. Seremela and Duncan had shared good conversations at group events, and she had hoped they might have begun to develop a friendship, but coming in person to check on her wellbeing went beyond anything she could have expected.

He cocked his head. "Are you okay?" he asked gently. "You haven't had a death in the family, have you?"

"No!" she blurted out. "No, I haven't. Duncan, I—this was so thoughtful of you. Thank you."

"Oh, good," he said. The set of his shoulders eased, and he gave her that crooked smile of his that was so damn charming. "Nobody has died, and you aren't angry with me for intruding. I count both those things as wins. Do you mind me asking what has happened? We're all transplants to Miami, and it's all too possible to feel cut-off and alone. Carling and I were both concerned you might need help but not feel comfortable enough to ask for it."

She groaned and gestured. "I just found out my niece ran away from home a few months ago. My sister has kept it under wraps all this time. She hired a detective to find Vetta—that's my niece—and now that he has tracked her down, we need to bring her home."

Duncan's gaze had grown intent as she talked. "I take it your niece is all right?"

"Yes, as far as I understand, she is," Seremela said.

"That girl's got a talent for finding trouble though, and if she can't find trouble, often she'll create it. I'm afraid I can't talk with you long. I'm on standby, and I'm getting ready to leave for the airport so I can take the first available flight out."

"Your sister must be grateful you're going with her to get Vetta."

Seremela shook her head. "Oh, my sister's not going to get Vetta."

Duncan's sleek dark brows lowered. "Excuse me?"

Seremela gave him a dry look. "Camilla can't face conflict," she explained. "I'm going to get Vetta by myself."

His frown deepened. "Forgive me again," he said. "I'm well aware of how intrusive this might seem, but I do not like the sound of that."

"Well, it is what it is." She twitched a shoulder. "Although I know how irritating that statement is to a lot of people too. Right now the most important thing is to get Vetta home safely, and that means moving as quickly as possible now that we know where she is. Everything else can be dealt with later."

As she talked, Duncan turned to look out the open balcony door. She didn't mind in the slightest. It gave her the opportunity to study his profile.

Slight lines carved the corners of his eyes and his expressive, well formed mouth. He must have been around thirty when Carling turned him at the height of the California Gold Rush in the mid nineteenth century.

While he would forever wear a young man's face, there were subtle telltale signs that spoke otherwise. He carried a certain gravitas in his presence that simply didn't exist in younger men. Somehow it held the weight of years and experience without seeming too heavy.

Oh, she did like him, so much. She twisted her fingers together and offered, "I also thought about asking the detective if he would go with me when I went to get her."

Duncan pursed his mouth. The small, thoughtful expression hollowed already lean cheeks and accentuated the strong line of his cheekbones. "Most detectives won't get physically involved, especially if it involves a family matter," he said. "The majority of detectives work on divorce documentation, do background checks and that sort of thing."

"I know," she said quietly. She had also thought about hiring someone who specialized in extracting people from cults, drugs and other subversive cultures. She just wasn't sure any professional interventionist would agree to handle something as trivial as Vetta's sheer bloody mindedness.

Vetta wasn't addicted or brain washed. She was just contrary to the bone. She was also twenty, which was especially unfortunate since that was well past the age of consent in most jurisdictions. Medusae aged so much more slowly than humans, and Vetta's emotional maturity was more like a young human teenager's than a grown adult.

"Where is your niece now?" he asked, glancing at her.

She closed her eyes and sighed. "She's at Devil's Gate."

"Devil's Gate?" He pivoted sharply to face her.

"I see you know of it," she said, her voice flat.

"Of course I know of it," he said. "Bloody hell."

Chapter Two

Law

D EVIL'S GATE. YES, Duncan knew of it.

That period of his life was etched indelibly in his mind. He had lived his last days as a human and his first nights as a Vampyre during the riotous Gold Rush in San Francisco. He would wake in the evenings, starving for fresh blood and newspapers. Gods, he had loved that time. It had been wild, greedy and anarchistic, and everyone had been a sculptor, carving out their futures and fortunes the best way they knew how.

He had followed the original news about Devil's Gate in the *Pacific Courier*. In June of 1850, a gold nugget had been discovered at Devil's Gate, which lay just north of Silver City in western Nevada. For ten years the entire area became the scene of frenetic mining. The gold rush in Nevada had been even wilder than the California Gold Rush, fueled by a thread of land magic that ran like liquid mercury throughout the desert mountains and rock.

Formed out of lava rock, Devil's Gate itself had been blasted wider to create a toll road on the route to

Virginia City. The narrow opening soon became notorious as a popular hideout for highwayman, and anyone who wanted to pass along the route safely had to travel armed.

Even with the last hundred and sixty years of searching and with modern surveying techniques, it was still possible today to stumble upon a vein of magic-rich metal. In eastern Nevada, the Nirvana Silver Mining Company had done just that when they had accidentally blasted open a passageway to a small pocket of Other land that held a magic-rich silver node.

A few months ago, in March, the news of the discovery had slammed through the media. The law was very clear about mining rights and ownership in Other lands. Even though the passageway was on the Nirvana company grounds, and even though there were no indigenous people living in the Other land, the mining company had no legal right to harvest the newfound vein of silver.

Succumbing to greed, the company owner had imported undocumented workers and held them against their will, forcing them to work in such inhumane circumstances that several had died. An Elder tribunal Peacekeeper on a routine mission had uncovered the crimes.

The magic that ran through the rock in Devil's Gate had never led to a full crossover passageway—at least not one that had ever been discovered or documented. But after what happened in Nirvana, that slight spark of land magic had been enough to ignite the imaginations of a great many people.

After all, if a crossover passageway leading to a magic-rich silver node could be uncovered so recently in Nirvana, who knows what one could discover in the witchy land at Devil's Gate? Perhaps there were slivers of previously undiscovered gold, or there might be more magic-rich silver, or even more buried passageways that led to Other lands.

Thousands of people, both Elder Races and humankind, converged upon the place. They chased gold and silver, magic and fool's dreams of sudden wealth.

Almost overnight a sprawling city of tents and RVs sprang up in Gold Canyon. By mid-April, nearly sixty thousand people had struck camp. At the end of May, the tent city had grown to over twice that size. Desperate for opportunity and a fresh start, illegal immigrants poured north from Mexico, while charlatans and schemers, sightseers, prostitutes, drug dealers and thieves poured in from all over the globe, creating a brawling mess that grew messier and more violent as the summer solstice came closer and the desert temperatures escalated accordingly.

The State of Nevada was caught completely off guard. Lawmakers struggled to come up with an effective way to deal with the situation, their resources already severely overburdened from a long economic downturn. They didn't have the manpower to police an entirely new city that had sprung up overnight.

The last Duncan had heard, the state had filed several appeals for help, with the Nightkind demesne in California, with the Demonkind demesne in Texas, and with the human Federal government.

The process had stalled under one essential question: under whose jurisdiction did the very expensive problem fall? If more than fifty percent of the population in the tent city were creatures of the Elder Races, then the jurisdiction—and responsibility for policing it—fell to the Elder Races demesnes. But nobody could answer the question, because nobody had conducted a Census. There hadn't been time.

And Seremela intended to walk all alone into that cesspool?

Duncan's jaw tightened as he looked down into her face. "This won't do, Seremela," he said, and this time he didn't even bother with an apology for intruding. Determination hardened his face and body. "It won't do at all."

A spark of amusement had entered her colorful, intelligent gaze. "If by 'it won't do,' you mean that Vetta can't be allowed to wreak havoc on the thousands of unsuspecting people at Devil's Gate, you would be right," she said. "That girl is like water running downhill. She can find the lowest common denominator in just about any situation."

"I think you know very well that's not what I meant," he said.

He had not met many medusae before her. They

were rare, comprising only a small fraction of the Demonkind population, and they also tended to be rather clannish.

Seremela was strange to him, and lovely, with fine-boned, feminine features and blue-green eyes that had vertical slits for pupils. She seemed on the small side for a medusa, which was around average height for a human woman, with a trim waist and rounded breasts and hips. Her skin was a pale creamy green that had a faint iridescent pattern that resembled the pattern on snakeskin, but he had touched her hand before on other occasions, and her warm soft skin felt entirely human. He loved her exotic beauty. Her snakes were frankly mischievous, and he loved them as well.

Most of all what drew him to her was her intelligence and her gentle nature. She was a medical doctor, a pathologist and an academician. Her snakes were poisonous, which did give her beauty a certain edge, but many creatures, like himself, were immune to their poison.

And in any case, she would have to be caught in a situation extreme enough that her snakes felt threatened to bite. Even the most quickly acting poisons took at least a few moments to act. In a physical struggle, those few moments could easily mean the difference between life or death.

She could be deadly, but she was also very vulnerable.

Unable to resist, he reached out to take her hand,

and she let him. He relished the sense of her slender warm fingers resting in his grip. She kept her neat, oval fingernails trimmed close, a practical choice for a medical examiner turned researcher. "You can't go to Devil's Gate all by yourself. It's too dangerous."

She did not protest nor did she appear to be angry at his presumptuous language. Instead, she stared at their hands as she pointed out, "My niece is there all by herself."

"Which, we can both agree, is not acceptable," he said.

The smile in her eyes dimmed, her expression tightened and she looked at the floor. "Well, there isn't any other option," she told him. "I spent half the night and much of this morning trying to figure out the best thing to do."

"There has to be some other way," he said.

"There isn't," she said, her voice turning flat again. "There's no legal recourse. The state can't even keep the area adequately policed. They certainly don't have the resources to send anyone in to find one person who I can guarantee doesn't want to be found. And frankly, I don't want to bully my sister into going with me. She'd only wring her hands, fall apart and be useless. Trust me, that would be much more trouble than it's worth."

"I understand," he said. He raised her hand and pressed his lips against her fingers. She froze, her startled gaze flashing back up to his. "But nevertheless I still can't let you go to Devil's Gate by yourself."

This time she did pick up on his language. "You can't let me," she repeated with a careful lack of emphasis.

He knew exactly what it sounded like, and he was entirely unrepentant for it. He stressed, "Not by yourself, Seremela."

Her shoulders drooped and she tried to pull her hand out of his. "While I understand that you mean well, I don't have time to argue with you," she said. "My taxi's coming in less than a half an hour, and I'm not finished packing yet."

"Cancel it," he told her, his fingers tightening on hers.

"Duncan—"

He pulled her closer until they stood toe to toe, and he looked deeply into her strange, beautiful eyes. "Cancel it," he repeated. "And take your time as you finish packing. I will sort out the quickest flight to Reno then come back to pick you up."

He could see from her puzzled expression that she still didn't quite get it. "I'm not sure what to say."

In light of the number of clues he had dropped, her confusion seemed remarkably innocent and was entirely adorable. He raised an eyebrow. "You don't have to say anything," he said. "Or better yet, figure it out while you finish packing. You can tell me whatever it is on the flight, since I'm coming with you."

A delicious warm rose color washed intoxicatingly underneath her creamy light green skin. "You are?"

"I am. Now, don't argue with me," he said as she took in a quick breath. He began to wonder just how far she would let him push her. In wondering where her boundaries might be, and what she might do should he cross them, he began to enjoy her even more than he had before. "Just do as I say."

She shut her mouth with an audible click. "Can't. Won't. Don't. You've used a lot of archaic-sounding prohibitives in the last fifteen minutes."

He could tell she wasn't really angry. She was, ever so gently, warning him not to go too far. It pleased him so much he ran the tip of a finger very lightly down her cheek. "You might have noticed, my dear," he murmured. "I happen to be a nineteenth century kind of a guy."

HE LEFT HER sputtering and rosier than ever, and he spent a pleasant ride in the elevator to the basement garage wondering what she would say to him when he picked her up. A few minutes later, he called Carling and Rune's house. Rune picked up.

Carling was a Vampyre, but Rune wasn't. Rune was Wyr, and just under a year ago he had been First sentinel for Dragos Cuelebre, Lord of the Wyr in New York, until he had mated with Carling. Rune and Carling had relocated to Miami, and for several months they had been gathering underutilized talent from across several different demesnes.

Now Rune and Carling were setting up an

international consulting agency so that they could put to use the talent they had gathered around them. Some parts of the agency, such as consultations with the Oracle, would be operated on a sliding scale fee, and other parts would be profit-based only. Carling must have told Rune about Seremela's email, or perhaps Rune had read it for himself.

"Seremela and I need to fly to Reno," Duncan told Carling's mate.

"Yo-okay," said Rune. "Duncan, you dog."

"You had to go there," Duncan said. He smiled to himself as he negotiated the afternoon traffic. He liked Rune. They had learned to work well together when they had traveled to the Dark Fae Other land of Adriyel to see Niniane Lorelle safely to her coronation as the Dark Fae Queen.

"Seriously, is everything all right?"

"I hope so. Seremela has a runaway niece who has ended up at Devil's Gate, of all places." He paused briefly as he listened to Rune mutter a curse. "We're going to extract her from the situation and escort her home to her mother."

"Anything we can do?"

One of the first acquisitions their brand new consulting agency had purchased was a private jet that could seat up to twelve people and that had the capacity for international travel. They were serious about the agency and were allocating enough money to set it up with top notch resources.

Of course Duncan was well aware that the plane also had the capacity to travel quite comfortably across the continental U.S.

"It would be nice," Duncan said, "to get to Nevada as quickly as possible before her niece has a chance to get hurt."

"Is this urgent enough to bargain away a favor to a Djinn?"

Duncan gave the question serious consideration. Most people had never even met a Djinn. Still fewer were able to draw a Djinn's attention long enough to bargain with one. Duncan and Seremela were acquainted with Khalil and could talk with him, but Khalil's Djinn sensibilities were such that he would probably see nothing wrong with bargaining with them for a favor in return. While the situation at Devil's Gate was unsafe and volatile, owing a favor to a Djinn could be an expensive and even more dangerous business over the long haul.

He said, "I don't think so. Still, we should get there quickly."

"I'll have the plane fueled and on the tarmac inside an hour," Rune said.

"Thanks, I appreciate it."

"I wish Seremela had felt comfortable enough to ask us herself."

"Borrowing a plane is quite a big favor to ask, Rune," Duncan told him. "And she's new to Miami and still feeling her way. Hell, we all are. It's just that some of us have known each other longer than others. Give her time."

"Good point. Let us know if there's anything else we can do."

"Will do." Duncan ended the call.

He was frowning when he reached his fifteen thousand square foot house. He would pack two bags. One of them would be a backpack filled with weapons, cash, a few toiletries and ways to keep himself protected from the sun. That would be the essential bag.

The other would be filled with luxuries like extra clothing, along with a securely encrypted laptop in case he found some time to get some work done. While he would also definitely pack a satellite phone as well, the land magic around Devil's Gate interfered with phone reception so they would have to plan on being self-sufficient.

They would have to drive to Devil's Gate from Reno, which meant they needed to rent an SUV. He made more calls to arrange a rental, including camping supplies, food and water for Seremela, and several cases of bloodwine. He tried to rent an RV, but there weren't any available on short notice within five hundred miles of Devil's Gate.

If retrieving Seremela's niece took longer than a few days, and if anything happened to his food supply, he would have to hunt for sustenance. Hopefully he would be able to find and pay for willing donors. If not, he would do what he had to do. He thought of the delectable healthy blush that had risen in Seremela's cheeks, and rather to his shock, his cock hardened in response.

He was an intelligent, educated and mature man who believed in law, in self control, and in regulating his emotions. He did not mix his appetites or confuse hunger for sustenance with sexual desire. He would not be that inconsiderate, either to his donors or to his lovers. Not even when a chaotic, sexy harpy had offered him a chance to taste her rare blood in exchange for sex had he given in to temptation.

But he also knew there were places and times where the law did not reach, and Devil's Gate was one of those places and one of those times. Apparently there were also times when a man's appetites became mixed, no matter how much self control he might try to exert over himself.

It had been some time since Duncan had done so, but he knew how to navigate through lawlessness. In fact he was looking forward to it again, and while he would have helped Seremela for decency's sake, no matter what, it certainly did not hurt in the slightest that she was so very beautiful, and he was intensely attracted to her.

No doubt she would be very grateful for everything he did. She might even offer to feed him, herself.

If she did, despite all of his carefully thought out principles, he would take what she offered. Hell, he would jump at the chance. His cock grew even harder as he thought of her bare, slender neck arched in invitation.

He thought of sinking his teeth into her soft skin while her breasts filled his hands, and his erection grew so tight it became painful.

Oh, Duncan, he thought. You had to go there too, didn't you? Rune had been teasing, but he'd also had the right of it. You are a lowdown dirty dog.

Chapter Three

The Dance

WHILE SEREMELA WAFFLED over what to pack, her iPhone pinged. She hurried into the living room to snatch it up from the coffee table.

She had received a text from Duncan. *Everything is set. We have transportation to Reno, also an SUV with supplies. I'll be there at noon to pick you up.*

An invisible weight lifted from her shoulders. She was intelligent and capable. She could have arranged transport. She could have retrieved Vetta on her own. But the fact that she didn't have to, that she had the kind of emotional support that Duncan had so generously offered her, was indescribably wonderful. It spoke of serious caring, and friendship.

The fact that she also found him heart-stoppingly sexy shouldn't factor into her thinking at all. She should be focused on the task itself, which was ensuring that her niece got home safely—whether Vetta wanted to or not.

And Seremela would be focused on the task, when it really mattered. For now, she felt young, and feeling that way at nearly four hundred years old was a kick. Her pulse raced like a giddy schoolgirl's.

She and Duncan would have hours of time alone. She could watch him in secret. Sometimes he would smile at her in that slightly crooked self-deprecating way that he had. He would talk with her, combining his intelligence with the sound of his gorgeous voice in a way that was so seductive to her. They might have as much as two or three days together. It seemed an extravagant fortune in stolen time.

Carefully she texted him back. *Thank you for everything.*

His response was immediate. *It's my pleasure. See you soon.*

Seremela checked her email messages and found a reply from Carling that the other woman must have sent even as Duncan drove to her apartment earlier. Of course Seremela could have as much time off as she needed, and she was to let Carling and Rune know if there was anything they could do to help.

Seremela had to smile. She didn't doubt for a minute that Carling had known very well what she was doing when she had shared Seremela's email with Duncan. Carling had already provided more help than Seremela could have hoped.

The weather changed drastically over the next hour, swirls of sunlit blue sky breaking through the ominous dark clouds. They would have to take care on route to the airport. Seremela had finished packing in plenty of time, and she had showered and changed for the trip into jeans and a sleeveless yellow, button-down cotton shirt.

She felt calm and optimistic by the time Duncan knocked on her door again—and then, of course, all of that went to hell. Her snakes spilled in a helter-skelter swirl around her shoulders. If they really had been dogs, she had no doubt they would have been barking and having a running fit.

Time to bite the bullet. She wasn't about to spend the next three or four days keeping the brats constantly under wrap under extreme desert heat, even though they totally deserved it. She squared her shoulders, marched over to the door and opened it.

"Hello, Seremela," said Duncan. "Have you had time to—?"

She caught one glimpse of him. He, too, had changed into an outfit very similar to hers, wearing jeans and a gray T-shirt that molded to his lean torso and muscled biceps. Previously whenever Seremela had seen him, he had always been the epitome of cool male elegance. It was shocking, somehow, to see him so casually dressed.

Or at least she thought it was. She didn't get a good enough look to be sure. Her snakes obscured her vision as they swarmed around her shoulders and over her head, shooting toward Duncan any way they could. The strength of their reaction surprised her and caught her off balance. She stumbled forward a step, which was all they needed.

Duncan began to laugh as her snakes wrapped

around his neck and his upper arms. He caught her under her elbows as she stumbled, and they stood staring at each other, entwined. Something electric sparked in his eyes. She didn't know what it was, but the strength of it affected her powerfully. Her skin flashed with heat.

"I'm sorry," she mumbled. "It's only—you know they just like you, and—"

"Don't apologize," he told her in a gentle voice. He touched her cheek with the fingertips of one hand. "Like I've told you, I enjoy them."

Others might thrill to the crash and thunder of tumultuous passion. For Seremela, the most lethal thing in the world was exactly this kind of gentleness, this type of moment. They stood near enough to each other that she could see how his dark eyes had dilated, a subtle enough change in color that if she had stood even a few feet away, she wouldn't have caught it. He looked at her intently, his face sharpened with that same electric expression that pierced through his gaze, yet he touched her as lightly as snowflakes drifting down to rest on her sensitive skin.

She was intensely aware of each of the four small points of contact, even more so because she could barely feel them, and they held so steady, so steady, as he looked deep into her eyes. That single, innocent touch was almost unbelievably erotic. The steady light contact said things, and the very fact that he paused so long meant that he made sure she heard it.

It said his exquisite gentleness was no accident. It

said he had to be intimately aware of the placement and position of her body to achieve such a delicate, butterfly touch. It said he touched her because he wanted to touch her, and that he knew how to be gentle and tender, that he was confident and didn't shy away from scrutiny, and that he could hold steady when he needed to.

It said he knew very well that she was clever enough to hear all of the nuances in his unspoken message.

Her breathing grew ragged. Her lips trembled as her snakes held him in position and he smiled into her eyes. And all he did was touch her cheek.

"Are you ready to go?" he said quietly, his fabulous, famous voice pitched for her ears alone.

And that was it, man, she just about came right there in her pants. The fact that she didn't was a miracle. She should be glad about it, since she could hope to maintain some semblance of dignity....

She glanced sideways at her snakes which had locked around him. One had wrapped around his biceps so far it was peering at her upside down, from underneath his arm.

Yeah well, she might not be able to maintain dignity exactly.

LET GO! she ordered. It was as stern a mental voice as she had ever used on them.

She must have startled them because they loosened and slipped back over her shoulders. Grateful, she took a deep breath and stepped back. She said aloud, somewhat hoarsely, "Yes, I'm ready."

He inclined his sleek, dark head with a smile, stepped inside and picked up her carry-on, while she looked around her apartment one last time, checked to make sure she had her iPhone, and shut and locked the door as they left.

Internally she was flipping rapidly through her Rolodex of teeming emotions. What to label this feeling? She had roared through embarrassment several minutes ago, so nah, that wasn't it. As they rode the elevator down to the garage in silence, she finally had to admit, she didn't know what she felt. She had never felt it before, so it wasn't in her Rolodex.

She did know the emotion held a large amount of shock and amazement.

Because *all he did was touch her cheek.*

And now all she could do was wonder, what else could he say in that silent, sensual language of his?

What poems could his fingers whisper as they danced across her skin?

What eloquent prose could he share with his body?

SHE HAD ASSUMED THEY would be flying out of the Miami International Airport and was surprised when Duncan drove them instead toward Kendall-Tamiami Executive Airport, thirteen miles southwest of downtown Miami. Breaking the silence for the first time since they had left her apartment, she said, "I didn't know there were any commercial flights out of this airport."

He gave her a brief smile. "There aren't, but there are corporate flights. We're not taking a commercial flight. We're using the agency plane."

"Oh, I see."

The possibility hadn't even crossed her mind, and she was frankly staggered. Rune and Carling had given her so much already. Carling had given her a papyrus sketch she had made in ancient Egypt, of a long-dead, half serpent, half human woman who, according to legend, had founded the medusa race. While the worth of the sketch didn't matter to Carling, the fact remained that it would still fetch a small fortune from a museum if Seremela ever chose to sell it. Then there was the new job, for which they paid her an extremely competitive salary, gave her a great benefit package and even paid for her relocation expenses. Now they gave her an unspecified amount of time off and were lending their agency plane.

When they returned, she would have to thank them properly, in person. The least she could do was have them over for supper. Carling could enjoy an excellent bottle of wine, and Rune certainly had a hearty enough appetite for several normal men combined.

Her gaze slid sideways to Duncan. Perhaps Duncan could join them. She smiled, feeling warm all over at the thought.

They parked, and Seremela glanced at the sky again as they exited the car. To the north, the sky had turned almost entirely blue. She could see the rays of sunshine spilling over the edge of dark clouds like laser beams. Her stomach tightened at the sight, and she turned to Duncan anxiously.

He glanced at the sky and gave her a calm smile. "It's all right. We've got a few more minutes. There's enough time to board."

"If you say so." She took her case as he handed it to her. Then he took his two cases, slammed the trunk and they strode toward the building. Once they were inside, she was able to take a deep breath again, but in order to board the Gulfstream jet, they had to go back outside again.

Duncan remained calm the entire time, and he never pulled out a cloak but he did take the stairway ramp to the plane at a lope just as sunshine spilled out over the northwestern border of the airport runway.

"Good gods," she muttered as he disappeared inside the plane. She glanced at the plane windows, noting that they were already lowered. His entire life was like this, a never-ending dance to avoid the sun. Feeling somewhat wrung out, she followed him at a slower pace up the ramp.

The pilot and her copilot were the plane's entire staff, and they greeted Duncan and Seremela cheerfully as they took their luggage to stow. Duncan held onto one piece of luggage long enough to pull out a laptop and a slim briefcase. He smiled at Seremela. "I hope you don't mind if I focus on work for a while."

"Of course not," she said. "This isn't a vacation. I

would have brought work too, if I thought I could concentrate enough to get anything done. Well, that, and half my job involves growing nasty things in petri dishes."

He laughed. "Thank you for not bringing your work with you."

She grinned. "You're welcome."

The plane had a couch, and after takeoff when Duncan settled to work at a table, Seremela gave into temptation and stretched out to rest. Her sleepless night had caught up with her. The copilot brought her a pillow and a blanket and she curled on her side, her snakes spilling down her body and coiling in the natural hollow made by the indentation of her waist.

She dozed, rousing slightly every time she heard Duncan's voice. Mostly he was arranging for his time out of the office for the next several days, but once she surfaced to wakefulness with a pulse of alarm.

She clenched without moving, and she knew all of her snakes were awake and coiled with readiness too. The plane's engine ran strong and smoothly, and all seemed normal. What was it that had woken her?

Then she heard it again, Duncan speaking in a voice so cold and sharp it speared through the silence in the cabin like a stiletto. "...the fact remains, Julian, Carling's house is on an island in an Other land. Further, you can only access the passageway to the island from the ocean. Do you think she chose any of this by accident? It is not in the Nightkind demesne, so it does not fall under your legal domain. We have been patient now for a year."

Wow, he was really angry at this Julian guy. Then realization jangled through her. Duncan wasn't talking to just any Julian, but to Julian Regillus, the Nightkind King and Carling's estranged progeny.

Duncan paused, clearly listening to whatever was said on the other end of the line. Then he said icily, "That's unacceptable. Carling's magical library is too dangerous. She doesn't trust anyone else to move it. She needs to move it herself, and you cannot continue to block her access to her own property." Another pause. "It's too late for that. She's done waiting. We've already filed a petition with the Elder tribunal. It's only a matter of time until the tribunal approves it."

Then another silence that stretched on, until she realized that Duncan wasn't pausing to listen but that the phone call had ended without goodbyes. Cautiously she peeked around the edge of the couch.

Anger etched the lines of Duncan's expression, turning him into a hard faced stranger. His dark eyes glittered, shards of black in his pale face. The gentle, urbane man she had become acquainted with and liked so well was nowhere to be seen, and what was left in his place was something entirely dangerous.

Then he caught sight of her peering around the arm of the couch, and the hardness in his expression eased.

She said, "I'm sorry. I overheard some of that."

He shook his head and sighed, running his hands through his hair until he actually looked rumpled. She frowned. Maybe that shouldn't seem as adorable to her as it did, especially after what she had just seen in his expression.

"No, it is I who should be apologizing—again—to you," he said. "I woke you, didn't I?"

She didn't bother to deny it but just regarded him steadily. "As soon as I realized who you were talking to, I should have done something to let you know I was awake, like gone to the lavatory."

Even though he didn't need to breathe, his humanity had not left him, she saw, as he blew out a breath. "You absolutely should not have done that," he said. "I didn't realize I would be transferred to Julian himself, or I never would have called. Then at that point the phone call took a dive straight into the toilet."

"Well, since the damage is done," she said, as she sat up. "If you don't mind me asking, why won't Julian let Carling have access to the island? Is it because he doesn't want her to have her library?"

"I don't think so," Duncan said. "It's useless as anything but a retreat. As an Other land, it's illegal for anyone from Earth to harvest anything from the island for commercial gain, and Carling has filed evidence that an intelligent indigenous winged species lives in the redwoods. And Julian doesn't give a damn one way or another about Carling's library. In fact, he insists that Carling send librarian witches to pack it all up and transport it. On the other hand, Carling insists—and she does have the legal right of it—that she have free access to her own house and that she sees to the transportation of the library personally."

"But he doesn't want to let her do that," she said.

"No, he doesn't," Duncan said. "Now that he's made his stance and exiled her, he doesn't want to allow Carling anywhere near the border of his demesne, especially at the crossover passageway for the island where it would be so easy for her to slip quietly into the Nightkind demesne. He certainly does not want to acknowledge that she has the right to come and go as she pleases."

She sat up and folded the blanket, and he slid out from the table where his work lay spread and walked over to sit beside her on the couch. Three of her snakes slipped over his shoulder to peer at him.

He smiled and held out his hand to them. They twined around his forearm as she confessed, "I always wondered how you felt about their estrangement."

"To be brutally fair, I can see both sides," he said. "Julian made some mistakes and trusted the wrong person, and last year Carling really had been dangerous to be around. I think they could actually get past it all if Julian was willing to submit to Carling's dominance again. But I also think something inside of him has broken, and he can't do that again. And I must take Carling's side in all of this."

The conversation had slipped squarely into Vampyre territory, and Seremela frowned, unsure about how comfortable she felt with the subject. She looked down at her hands as she said carefully, "The bond between a Vampyre maker and her progeny is something difficult to understand from the outside. I suppose you must take Carling's side, mustn't you?"

"Do you mean, did Carling order me to take her side?" Duncan asked. He smiled at her, all vestiges of the hard edged stranger gone. "No, she didn't. She wouldn't do that. I must take Carling's side because I love her, and I agree with her stance more than I agree with Julian's. But that doesn't mean I can't see Julian's side of things too."

His ability to see all perspectives of a situation would be one of the things that made him such an outstanding attorney. She had to smile. It could make him an outstanding friend as well. Or enemy. It was one more thing that she liked so much about him. His quiet, incisive intelligence had its own kind of bite.

He was still speaking. He said, "And there's also a big difference between me and Julian."

"What difference is that?" she asked, growing fascinated despite her initial discomfort.

A thrill ran through her nerve endings as Duncan took one of her hands and played with her fingers. "Thousands of years," he told her. "You see, I accept Carling's rule over me. She made me, and I'm young enough to remember how I felt when I agreed to that. Yes, she has the Power to force me to her will, but in the last hundred and seventy years, she has almost never done so, and she never has without having a compelling reason for it. But Julian was turned at the height of the Roman Empire. He and Carling, and Rune too—the three of them are different from us."

"Us?" she repeated in surprise. "As in you and me?"

"Yes, as in you and me," he said.

She smiled at him, amused. "Do you realize I'm probably close to two hundred years older than you?"

He grinned. "I was thirty when I was turned, so if you're over three hundred and fifty, then yes, you are. But the age difference between you and me is a drop in the bucket when you look at millennia. They are all so much older than we are. I think it makes them fundamentally different in some way. And Julian is very dominant. Carling has never changed anyone against their will, so he must have once, long, long ago, agreed to her dominance, but I think he has chafed under her Power for a very long time. Imagine what it must have been like for him when it looked like she was dying."

She frowned. "I suppose, even if he cared for her, in some ways it must have felt like a relief."

"That is how I see it," Duncan said. "For many years they worked well in partnership with each other. They played off each other's strengths very well. But she didn't die when she was supposed to, and he wasn't freed. Now he can't stand the thought of being under her Power again. And if they ever saw each other in person, she could potentially force him to her will—he is her progeny, after all. I don't think Julian ever hated Carling before. But I think maybe he has learned to hate her now."

"The way you describe it, it sounds like they're in the middle of some kind of duel."

"That's a good way to describe it," Duncan said. "Only this duel may take centuries to play out."

She shuddered and curled her fingers around his. "It disturbs me to think about you possibly getting caught in the middle of their—" What should she call it? Disagreement sounded far too simple. "Their clash of wills."

"Oh well," he said wryly. "'Every family has its ups and downs.'"

Seremela went into delighted shock. "Did you just quote Katherine Hepburn as Eleanor of Aquitaine from *The Lion in Winter*, or was that an accident?"

He smiled into her gaze. "What if I did?"

Under the full bore force of such close contact, her breathing grew restricted. "I loved that movie."

"I did too. I've also had a lot of reason to quote it through recent years." He pressed a kiss against the back of her hand. "Speaking of families, I think we're getting ready to land. Once we get the SUV and our supplies, it should take us about an hour to get to Devil's Gate. Then we can collect your niece and take her home."

She chuckled. "You make it sound so easy."

"After Carling and Julian? You bet, this is easy," Duncan said.

Seremela shook her head at him and gave him a pitying grin. "You say that only because you haven't met Vetta yet."

Chapter Four

Death

B Y THE TIME the plane had landed at the Reno-Tahoe Airport and they had disembarked, met with the travel agency Duncan had used to book the SUV, signed for the vehicle and then inspected the food, water and camping supplies to make sure they had everything they needed, most of the daylight had slipped away. Duncan drove and once they reached US-395 S, traffic opened up and they made good time.

Reno was like many cities in the desert where they seemed to leave the populated area all at once. As he picked up speed on the open highway, he asked Seremela, "Do you mind if I roll down the windows?"

"Not at all," she said, although he noticed that she glanced at the western sky.

The sun hadn't completely set but it was low enough on the horizon that at times it was obscured by the hills in the west. The colors of the summer desert evening were large splashes of deepening tan and gold sliced with elongated black shadows, and the departing day left fiery banners of rose, lavender and purple strewn across the sky.

Duncan touched the controls embedded in the driver's seat door, and the windows lowered several inches. Nevada could reach triple digits in the heat of the day in June, but the heat cooled rapidly in the evening and the fresh air merely felt pleasantly warm.

After a moment, he said, "You know, some Vampyres are rigid about eschewing daylight hours. They will not step outside of shelter until the sun has completely set, and they are well under cover by sunrise every morning. It happens a lot with older Vampyres. Some of them turn agoraphobic and almost never leave their shelters. I'm not sure why. Perhaps as time goes by, they feel the odds stacking against them for having a fatal accident."

She stirred. A few of her snakes had lifted to the open window, tongues flickering to taste the desert air. To his amusement, a few others rested on his right shoulder. "I guess I can understand that," she said. "Sunlight is so lethal for you."

He nodded. "We live side-by-side with death. It's always there, just a few hours ahead or behind us, around the corner, or a few steps out from the shelter of a roof. But when Carling turned me, I told myself that I would not become like those other Vampyres. I would take sensible precautions but never live in fear."

"What kind of precautions do you take?" she asked.

"Well, for one thing, I do have a large house," he

said. "If I have to take shelter from the sun, I refuse to feel cramped when I do. All the windows have metal shutters that operate on a timer. They automatically close and lock from sunrise to sundown." The system took a manual override code to open them any time during the day. Nobody was letting sunlight spear into Duncan's home without his express permission.

"I've heard of those shutters," she said. "Don't Carling and Rune have the same kind of thing in their new home too?"

"Yes." He slanted a glance at her. "And I can't tell you how exciting it was when full spectrum sunscreen became available. I would slather it all over and comb it through my hair before sunscreen spray made that a lot easier. For a while I looked like a throwback to a 1940s mafia kingpin."

She chuckled and relaxed. "So it really helps?"

"It does," he told her. "It protects against accidentally coming in contact with direct sunlight, and it can give a Vampyre up to ten minutes of leeway time to find shade. It has limitations—no Vampyre in his right mind would totally trust his life to waterproof sunscreen and go swimming in the daytime. But it's especially effective at dawn and dusk, like now, when any sunlight is indirect and fading fast. And I always wear it whenever I go out in the daytime."

"Good to know," she said. "I suppose you use sunscreen clothing too."

"Of course," he said. "All of my clothes are made of

UPF 50+ material that blocks up to 98 percent of UV rays. On its own, it's not enough, but it is added insurance. And whenever I have to go out in the day, I always keep a cloak nearby, which is also made with sunscreen cloth."

As he gave her the information, he could see that her natural scientific curiosity had taken over and her nervousness eased. The silence that fell between them after that was thoughtful and companionable, and he smiled to himself.

He'd have to be a liar or blind to claim he wasn't affected by her beauty, because he was, but what really engaged his interest was her quick mind. It was such a goddamn pleasure to seduce an intelligent woman.

Because that's what he was going to do. Seduce her. Yeah, this lowdown dirty dog was going on the hunt. He would coax her into sharing her secrets of warmth and passion while candlelight gilded the insanely gorgeous iridescence of her skin. Just the thought of it made his fangs descend, and the whip of the night air turned exhilarative as his groin tightened painfully.

His urges and feelings were in an uproar every time he thought of her or let his imagination run unleashed. So much for compartmentalizing his appetites.

Maybe he would bite her.

Maybe she would bite him.

He kept his mouth shut and his jaw clenched, and he was savagely glad for the deep shadows in the car, and that somehow he managed to keep the vehicle steady on the road.

Maybe she would bite him all over.

Goddamn.

DESPITE THE FACT THAT they had left the city behind and drove in full desert, traffic picked up again when he turned onto State Road 342. Soon a glow of light shone like a dome against the darkness of the night sky, and Duncan knew they were getting close. He followed the flow of vehicles which slowed to a crawl on the two-lane highway, until they came upon a shadowed wall of rock that rose on either side of the road.

"There it is," Seremela whispered.

An elusive tingle of land magic brushed his senses, along with a sense of other magic sparks flaring in the distance.

Their headlights flashed on a historical marker. Duncan caught a glimpse of the text but it was too small and dense to read. Several yards past the marker, a large, clapboard sign had been erected. Written in orange neon spray paint, the words jumped off the board.

The sign read:

Devil's Gate

Pop: ~~28,993 suckas~~

~~69,345~~

Past ~~100,000~~

Who the fuck knows?

He glanced at Seremela who looked back at him, wide-eyed. Then they both burst out laughing. Seremela said, "Even if the tent city is outlandishly bloated, medusae are rare enough that it won't be hard to find her. People tend to take notice when we are around."

"I'm sure they do," Duncan said. Giving in to impulse, he trailed his fingers down her warm, slender forearm and clasped her hand. Her breath caught, the tiny sound all but inaudible, but with his sharp Vampyre's hearing, he heard it easily.

She didn't pull away. Instead she turned her hand over and held his, palm to palm. He rubbed his thumb along the smooth skin on the back of her hand and wondered how she could sit there so calmly, because good gods, he was on fire all over for her, and she seemed completely unaware of the fact. He knew he had a good courtroom face, but he didn't know it was that good.

He drove one-handed, staying sedately in a line that crept toward the tent city at ten miles an hour. A few trucks pulled away and drove off over open land, but without knowing the terrain, he judged it best to follow the main stream of vehicles for now.

They were being stopped up ahead by a hulking troll who then directed them toward the right where they parked in a line. When it came his turn, Duncan released Seremela's hand and rolled his window down further.

The SUV creaked as the troll laid a hand on the roof and bent down to peer inside at them with small eyes and an incurious expression on his gray rock-like face. "Parking in our lot is three hundred a night," the troll rumbled. "Cash only."

Duncan's eyebrows raised. "Their lot." If any of them actually owned this piece of land, he was Pee-wee Herman.

"Three hundred dollars!" Seremela exclaimed, leaning forward. "A night?"

The troll gave her an indifferent glance. "You want to keep your car from being stolen? You want to keep your stuff, and all your tires too? That'll be three hundred dollars. In advance. You don't like it, lady, go park somewhere else, and good fucking luck with that, 'cause you're gonna need it."

For three hundred dollars a night, Duncan could get a room at one of the best hotels in San Francisco, one of the most expensive cities in the world. He shook his head and shifted in his seat to pull out his wallet.

"Duncan!" Seremela exclaimed telepathically. *"That's highway robbery."*

"Of course it is," he said. *"The troll and his organization probably vandalize and steal from anyone who doesn't use their parking lot. But if it keeps our supplies untouched and we can get away trouble free, it will be worth it."*

He pulled cash out of his wallet and offered it to the troll. The massive fingers closed over one end of the bills and tugged, but Duncan held on to them until the troll looked at him in exasperation. He said softly, "Anything happens, and I'm holding you personally responsible.

Not anybody else. You, bucko."

Maybe the troll finally took a good look at his face and recognized him. Trolls were Nightkind creatures too, and Duncan was, after all, extremely well known. Or maybe something in Duncan's voice got to him. Whatever it was, the troll masticated his massive jaw as if he chewed on something sour, but he muttered, "Nuthin's gonna happen."

"Very good," Duncan said. He let go of the cash and flicked two twenty dollar bills out of his wallet. "After we park, we're going to need reliable information. Where?"

"Down Main Street, north side," said the troll. "Look for the pharmacist. Name's Wendell. He'd sell pics of his mother's tits to the highest bidder. But they'd really be of his mother's tits." As Seremela stared, the troll lifted his rocky shoulders. "What can I say, guy's got a code. Sort of."

Duncan bit back a smile. "He your boss?"

"Yeah." The troll patted the roof of the SUV, straightened and lumbered back a step. "Now git outta here."

Duncan drove the SUV gently over the rough, pitted ground toward the end of one row of vehicles where a ghoul in an orange reflective vest stood, flashing them with a flashlight.

"I brought cash too," Seremela said. "I'll pay you back."

"Let's not worry about that right now," Duncan said. "It's unimportant. Let's just focus on getting your niece."

"Okay." She stayed silent for a moment as he parked the SUV. Then she said, "Wendell."

"The pornographer pharmacist," Duncan said, deadpan.

"It's not funny."

"Of course it's not," he said.

A soft, odd noise escaped her. It sounded a lot like hot air hissing out of a tea kettle. He looked at her suffused face, found her looking back at him, and then they both burst out laughing again.

He pulled the emergency brake and killed the engine. "Let's go see what Wendell has to say for himself."

"Okay," Seremela said, eyes dancing, "but if he tries to sell me a picture of his mother's tits, I'm so out of there."

Duncan laughed again. "Trust me, I'll be right on your heels."

They both sobered as they climbed out of the SUV. Duncan said, "The troll spoke the truth, but we should both keep a light pack with us just in case. This would not be a kind place to be stranded in without resources."

She nodded, her expression turning grim. She had a large soft bag with a shoulder strap, and she rifled through the contents and shifted over a few items from her carry-on. The last thing she added was a bottle of water. Then she pulled the shoulder strap over her head, lifted her snakes out of the way and settled it firmly across her torso.

Duncan's bag of essentials, with the weapons, money

and sun protections, was a leather backpack. He pulled out a Beretta 9mm and a five inch hunting knife on a belt. After strapping the pack to his back, he buckled on the knife belt and tucked the gun into the waist of his jeans, making sure the butt was well visible.

Seremela's gaze lingered at his waist when he turned to her, but she said nothing about the weapons. She did not carry an obvious weapon, but he noticed that she did not tie back her snakes. Usually she bound them back loosely with a simple scarf at the base of her neck, as though they were dreadlocks. That allowed them to move around but limited their range of reach. Without them restricted in any way, she looked wilder, more feral and exceedingly deadly.

He heartily approved. He asked, "Okay?"

She nodded again. Face calm, eyes sharp. Gods, this woman was hotter than Death Valley in July.

He couldn't resist touching her again. He cupped her cheek and rubbed his thumb gently along the soft, plush arc of her lips. Her expression softened, and the look she gave him was filled with equal parts tenderness and amazement. He wanted to ask her what caused her to look so surprised when he touched her with affection. He wanted to kiss her slowly and savor that first, intimate taste of her.

Hunger hissed along his nerve endings and turned aggressive. Her mouth would be so soft, the tender flesh giving way under his. He wanted to coax her lips apart and enter her with his tongue, and just the thought of deepening the kiss was so sexual his groin tightened.

Someone shouted nearby, splintering the moment. Frowning, he glanced around at the dust filled parking lot then he offered Seremela his hand. She took it.

"After this is over and we get back to Miami," he asked, "where are we going to go for our first date?"

Half a dozen of her snakes rose up to stare at him, and the nictating membranes snapped shut over Seremela's eyes. Then opened. Then shut. And opened. She blinked rapidly and it stopped. "First date?"

He wondered what that meant. Perhaps she got sand in her eyes. He asked, "Will you go out with me when we get back? I like the opera. But I like rock concerts too, and I'm a sucker for a good movie."

Her delighted smile was truly one of the loveliest expressions he had ever seen on her face. "Yes," she said. "I like all of that too, but I especially like the opera."

"Perfect," he said with satisfaction. "It'll give us something to look forward to."

At the time, he had no idea how much that would matter.

Hand-in-hand, together they walked into Devil's Gate.

It was everything he had expected, and more: dirty, stinky, unpredictable and overcrowded. The night was windless, and smoke from campfires hung in the air, thick with the scent of cigarette smoke, cooking meat and onions.

The scene threw him into a cascade of memories. He remembered how incredulous he felt when he found out that his legal work had come to Carling's attention. She had still been Queen of the Nightkind then, and she courted him with the wily patience of a professional politician and all the wisdom of a seasoned courtesan, until they had reached an agreement, about business and about other things.

His last meal before she changed him had been a sixteen ounce porterhouse steak, medium rare, with fried potatoes, apple pie and cheddar cheese, and a Guinness.

He remembered each detail as if it were yesterday. The meat had been so juicy and tender, he could cut it with his fork, and the potatoes had been crisp, salty with butter and a rich golden brown. The apple pie had been both tart and sweet, the tang of the sharp cheddar its perfect complement, and damn, that Guinness had been frothy and yeasty, like a satisfying novel for the taste buds, telling its dark, full-bodied and soul-nourishing story with every swallow. He had eaten until he thought he would burst.

Even though he still dreamed about that meal, the real thing would turn his stomach now, and while the present day camp brought back vivid memories, there were plenty of differences too.

The hellish red glows from the flames were interspersed with the cold, thin illumination from LED camping lanterns. Different kinds of music clashed, most of it blaring from boom boxes, but the sound of a few instruments, a guitar, a fiddle and drums, carried the piercing, startling sweetness of live passion.

Painted prostitutes, both men and women, walked the "streets" between the tents, campers and a few mobile office buildings. Humans, Elves and Light Fae, Demonkind and Wyr, and of course, the Nightkind were out in force. Vampyres prowled the area, smiling white smiles, drawn by the lawlessness and the lure of so much living blood packed into one space. Duncan backed them off silently with a glittering look. The Vampyres took one look at his hard face and melted into the crowd.

The tent city was a melting pot with the burner turned on high. At any minute he expected a fight to break out, and he wasn't disappointed. They had to sidestep two brawls as they navigated to "main street," the largest pathway that lay between camps.

He didn't pretend to himself that he was the only reason they remained unmolested. People took one look at Seremela, with her set expression, sharp gaze and snakes raised and wary, and they gave both of them a wide berth. When a drunk stumbled into her path and startled her, all her snakes whipped around and hissed at him, scaring him so badly he pissed himself as he ran away.

Duncan murmured to Seremela, "The California Gold Rush was so much more charming than this. I'm sure it was."

She glanced at him sardonically. "And I'm sure you

have swamp land in Florida you'd like to sell me."

He grinned and said to a tired looking, sunburned human, "We're looking for the pharmacy. Do you know where it is?"

The human's gaze passed over him and lingered on Seremela. "Five or six camps down," she said. "It's one of the fancy ones. Hard to miss."

"Thanks."

"Wonder what she means by fancy," Seremela muttered.

They discovered the answer to that soon enough as they found one of the few mobile buildings several campsites down. A simple sign that said "Wendell's" hung outside the door. The pale, cold light of LED lamps glowed through the window, and the door was propped open to the night air. Wendell's was open for business.

Normally Duncan always invited a lady to go first through the door, but normal wasn't a definition that applied to this place. He stepped in first and looked around quickly, one hand on his gun. Inside, the mobile building was crowded with metal shelves filled with merchandise, anything from canned goods, tampons, toothpaste, aspirin and other pain relievers, and first aid supplies to other, more potent supplies.

Duncan's sharp glance took in the bottles of OxyContin, Percocet and Demerol in a glass, locked cabinet behind a counter. He had no doubt that the right price, not a prescription, would be the key that would open up that cabinet. It also had a shelf of baggies filled with marijuana, some rolled and some loose, and a couple of shelves filled with dark brown tincture bottles, homeopathic concoctions that glinted with sparks of magic.

There were other people in the building. A few were obviously shoppers who took one look at Duncan and Seremela and then slipped out the open door. Duncan kept track of them until the last had left, but the main part of his attention was focused on the two people behind the counter.

One of them was a tall, dangerous looking Light Fae male, his curly blond hair shaved close to his skull, which made his pointed ears seem even longer. He wore two shoulder gun holsters over a tank top that bared a lot of golden brown skin. He watched Seremela with a flat, unfriendly gaze, resting a hand on one of his guns.

Duncan's jaw tightened. He did not like the sight of that. He turned his attention to the other person behind the counter, a short, slight human male with sharp eyes and a rather plain, aesthetic face. The male was easily the most intelligent person Duncan had laid eyes on since they arrived.

He said, "You must be Wendell."

"You're a quick one," said Wendell. "Hence the sign outside my door." He opened the foil wrap on a piece of Nicorette gum and popped it in his mouth, while his gaze took in everything about Duncan in one glance. "I recognize you. I know who you are." He turned and dissected Seremela appearance. "You got here just in time for the execution, but I'm afraid bringing a lawyer even as famous as he is won't do you any good."

Everything inside Duncan went cold and quiet when the other man said execution.

Seremela looked at the pharmacist blankly. "Excuse me?"

Wendell's thin eyebrows rose. "You're here about the Tarot reader, aren't you? The one who offed Thruvial."

If anything, Seremela looked even more confused and disturbed. "I have no idea what you're talking about."

"Eh, my mistake," Wendell said, shrugging. "I thought since you were a medusa that was why you were here. Guess I'm as guilty of racial profiling as anybody else."

Duncan took a step forward, and the Light Fae muscle matched him step for step. He ignored the other male and said to the pharmacist, "Do you know how many medusae are here in Devil's Gate?"

Wendell scratched the back of his neck. "Aside from your companion, there's only one that I know of—the Tarot reader. Young girl maybe twenty years old, wears Goth makeup, got a mouth on her."

"Goth makeup? Oh gods, Duncan," Seremela said, her creamy skin going chalky. "He's talking about Vetta."

Fuck. *Fuck.*

"Yeah, that's her name," said Wendell. His sharp

gaze had turned curious and more than a little avid. "I'll give you this much information for free, since it's common knowledge anyway. They say she poisoned a man a couple days ago. Someone who was very important here. They're going to hang her at dawn."

Chapter Five

The Depths

PANIC AND DISORIENTATION sank claws into Seremela and wouldn't let her go.

Vetta was to be hanged? For poisoning someone?

She couldn't drag in a deep enough breath and struggled for air as she stared at the human and his Light Fae bodyguard.

The Light Fae bruiser stared back at her, his cynical expression turning wary. He took a couple steps back and drew his gun.

"Leash your dog," Duncan said sharply. "He's about to get stupid."

What dog? Duncan moved so fast he blurred, crowding her back against a wall. Seremela stared at him blankly. What the hell was he doing?

When he stopped, he stood between her and the Light Fae, and belated understanding slammed into her—he was shielding her with his body.

At the same moment the nerdy human snapped, "Holster it, Dain."

Lean, strong fingers came under her chin, and Duncan forcibly turned her face toward him. "Don't look at him," Duncan said to her in a quiet voice. "Look at me."

She tried to focus on him. That was when she realized all her snakes were hissing at the Light Fae. Her panic had turned them deadly. She could feel them, roused and wanting to bite, and as she looked over Duncan's shoulder, she could tell that the Light Fae male knew it.

"At me, Seremela," Duncan whispered gently.

Her attention shifted back to him. He raised a hand and stroked it along a few of the snakes, and they quit hissing and wrapped around his forearm. Even though his back was turned to an unknown male with his gun drawn, Duncan looked calm, his dark gaze steady.

As soon as he knew he had gotten her attention, he smiled at her. *"They're not going to hang her,"* he said telepathically. *"We won't let them."*

She calmed, marginally. They were only two people in an overcrowded, dangerous and unknown place. Maybe it was ridiculous to believe him. Certainly it was neither sensible nor logical, but she did.

Impulsively she reached up to touch his lean cheek, more of the snakes reaching for him, and his gaze warmed. *"Duncan, I don't know what he's talking about,"* she said. *"Vetta isn't a Tarot reader, and she might be a total contrary shit, but she's not a* murderer. *That's insane. If—if by any chance she did kill someone, she wouldn't have had any other choice."*

He frowned. *"We need to ask some questions now. Whatever he says, we're going to make this right. Okay?"*

She nodded jerkily. *"Okay."*

He took her hand and kissed her fingertips, then carefully disengaged himself. Only then did he turn around to face the pharmacist and his Light Fae guard, who had holstered his gun.

All of her snakes had calmed as she had calmed. She gathered them to her and nudged them behind her shoulder as Duncan said, pleasantly, "Let's start this conversation over, shall we?"

Wendell regarded them both with narrowed eyes. "Fine, but you're scaring away my paying customers, so your free sample is over," he said, chewing gum. "You want to know anything else, you gotta pay. Standard 411 rate is ten dollars a minute, not including additional rates for premium intel."

Anger sparked in Seremela at the human's callousness. She had never in her life wanted to hurt another creature, but she was pretty sure she could hurt this one. *Just one bite,* she thought as she fixed a cold, level gaze on him. *All it would take is one, and your heart rate would slow, your skin would turn dry and flake off and you would be scared, nauseated and fucking miserable for a week. And I think I would like that very much.*

Even as she thought it, a single snake slipped over her shoulder and rose to the level of her cheekbone. It too stared at Wendell unblinkingly, until the human shifted on his stool and looked away.

Aw, she'd made him squirm. Yee-fucking-haw.

Duncan slipped his hands in his jeans pockets, standing relaxed. "Your rate's unimaginative but doable," he said.

The human's thin mouth tilted sourly, and he shifted again. "What the fuck do you mean by that?"

"There are much more valuable things than cash, Wendell," Duncan said. "Like alliances, protection and immunity."

Wendell's eyebrows rose. "You think you could offer me protection or immunity? You've barely set foot in this place. You have no social equity here, Vampyre. You don't know the Power brokers, and you have no alliances. You know nothing."

"The world is a much wider place than this dusty little pile of tents," Duncan said. He gave the human a cold smile, and a touch of a whip entered his voice, precisely balanced just so with a delicate lash of contempt. "But no worries, Wendell. If you want money, you'll get money. Tell us what happened, with details, names and times."

Wendell paused, regarding Duncan with equal parts greed and caution, and Seremela could tell he was rethinking the last few minutes. Then the pharmacist said, "There may not be any law here, but there is a balance of Power. Or there was, until one of the Power brokers was killed yesterday. Things are a bit destabilized at the moment."

"Who were the Power brokers, and what did they control?" Duncan asked. "You're not one of them."

"Nah," said Wendell as he glanced at his watch. "My motive is profit, not power. I'm strictly in parking and pharmaceuticals, with a side interest now and then in information. The real Power brokers in Devil's Gate are hard core. There's an Elf with an affinity to Earth. Caerlovena is her name. She's got a lock on most of the diggers. Then there's a Djinn, Malphas, who has a lock on all the casinos, and I mean all of them. And until yesterday, there was Cieran Thruvial, who locked on prostitutes and protection. All the shops and vendors owed him a cut of their take."

"Cieran Thruvial," Duncan said. Surprise flickered in his gaze. "I know that name."

Seremela shook her head. Inside she was reeling again. "That can't be right," she said. "I don't see Vetta turning to prostitution. I guess she could have, but I just don't see it."

Wendell shrugged. "Well, the girl read Tarot, or at least that's what her tent sign said. She charged for quarter hour and half hour readings. She did a good business too, from what I heard. I don't know if she was turning tricks on the side or not, but like a lot of other shop keepers, she owed Thruvial protection money. They had a tempestuous relationship and argued a lot in public. I gotta say, it seemed real intimate."

"Where is she now?" Seremela asked, the words scraping in her dry, constricted throat.

"Malphas is holding her until dawn," Wendell said, and for the first time since they met him, something like sympathy crept into his gaze. "Scary dude, that Djinn. I'm not sure what he cares about, if anything."

"Thruvial is a Fae name," Duncan said abruptly. "Was this Cieran Thruvial Dark Fae?"

This time, both Wendell and his guard shifted their attention to Duncan, their expressions sharpening. Speaking for the first time, the guard said, "Yes."

Wendell asked, "You knew him?"

Duncan's face had turned expressionless. He said, "I met him once."

"Where?" The pharmacist looked avid again.

Duncan gave him a sardonic smile. "That's not part of our agreement, Wendell. Where's the best place to find Malphas?"

Wendell made a face but said, "Much as he hangs anywhere, I guess it would be Gehenna—that's the name of his main casino. Get it? Devil's Gate—Gehenna. Ar ar ar, right?"

Duncan's dark gaze shifted to her. He asked the pharmacist, "What do we owe you?"

"You're not going to ask me how to find Gehenna?" Wendell asked.

Duncan shook his head. "We don't need you anymore."

"If I were you, I wouldn't be so quick to say that," Wendell said. "With Thruvial dead, things are shifting. People are making a grab for his territory, and a couple of them are strong magic users. You don't know who to watch out for, or where to go. You still don't know anything."

"Now you're trying too hard," Duncan told him. He pulled out some cash and laid it on the counter. "I make it just under fifteen minutes. Keep the change." He turned to Seremela, his expression softening. "Let's go."

She nodded and stepped out of the door, and he followed.

Wendell called after them, "You're making a mistake if you think you don't need me."

Duncan shook his head. Once they were outside, he offered Seremela his hand. She took it. His grip was like the rest of him, steady, calm and cool. She gripped it tightly and took a deep breath. The smoke scented night air seemed so much fresher than it had before they had stepped into Wendell's shop.

"What a scurvy little bug," she said between her teeth.

"I know. I want to squash him."

He pulled her around to face him, cupping her elbows in the palms of his hands while he watched the crowd behind her. After a quick glance at his face, she did the same, watching what happened at his back. The red-tinged light from various campfires was indirect. Nearby someone laughed, a sharp sound abruptly cut off. Magic tinged the air, mingling with the physical smells of spilt whiskey and other sour odors.

"Would you leave if I asked you to?" he asked

telepathically.

She glanced at his shadowed face quickly. He looked as casual and indifferent as if they were talking about the weather. A few choice responses occurred to her, but she saw too many reasons for why he asked what he did.

In the end she just simply said, *"No."*

He didn't look surprised. He nodded and rubbed his thumbs along the sensitive skin at the inside of her elbows, but she didn't think he was aware of what he was doing.

"The thing that bothers me is the Djinn," he said and frowned. *"Well, there's more than a few things that bother me."*

"Who was Thruvial?" she asked.

He met her gaze. *"Do you remember that I traveled last year with Carling to Adriyel for Niniane Lorelle's coronation?"*

"Yes," she said.

She wasn't likely to forget it.

Adriyel was the Dark Fae Other land, and last year had been eventful for the Dark Fae demesne. Dragos, the Lord of the Wyr, had killed Urien, the Dark Fae King, when Urien kidnapped Dragos's mate. Then the heir to the throne, Niniane Lorelle, who had been living under Dragos's protection, had to travel to Adriyel to claim her birthright. Along the way, Niniane had survived two assassination attempts in Chicago. Seremela had been the medical examiner who conducted an autopsy on the bodies of the would-be assassins.

The Wyr sentinel warlord Tiago had left his position in the Wyr demesne in New York to travel with Niniane and protect her. As far as the public knew, he now worked for the new Queen as her chief of security, but privately, those who knew the couple also knew that he had mated with Niniane.

Since that time, news from Adriyel had come out in snippets interspersed with weeks of silence. A few months after her coronation, the new Dark Fae Queen had imprisoned several noblemen and tried them for crimes committed against the crown, including treason, conspiracy, the regicide of her father and the murders of the rest of her family. Shortly after the trials, the conspirators had been executed.

A short time after, around January or so, Adriyel had officially opened its borders to tourism and open trade. Still, six months later, it was rare to see Dark Fae in the general public.

Seremela asked, *"Did you meet Thruvial in Adriyel?"*

"Yes, briefly," Duncan said. *"Thruvial was a nobleman, and I was just a part of Carling's entourage, so he and I had no reason to strike up a conversation. But I have a good memory for names and faces, and I remember him at the coronation and the celebration afterwards. Why would he come here, of all places?"*

Now he had her frowning as well. Urgency pounded in her veins. She needed to get to her niece. Vetta had finally bitten off more than she could chew, and the poor little shit had to be scared out of her mind. Sometimes people had to hit rock bottom before they could change. If that was true, Seremela didn't think there was any lower Vetta could go than sitting in the dark tonight, all alone, while she waited for her own execution.

But as much as Seremela wanted to barge over to Gehenna, Duncan was right to pause and assess the situation. They needed clear heads and to understand as much as they could about what was really going on, and part of that meant trying to understand the victim and why he had been killed.

She said, *"The Dark Fae are famous for their metallurgy. Maybe the possibility of finding a node of magic-rich metal lured him here, especially now that trade has opened up between Adriyel and the rest of the world."*

"Maybe, but if that was the case," Duncan said, *"why didn't Thruvial send servants or employees? Why come himself? And once he got here, why did he get involved in trafficking, and not excavation and mining?"*

"I don't know," she said, as frustration welled up.

His grip tightened. He repeated, *"But what really bothers me is the Djinn's presence here, and his involvement. Seremela, if you left, you could reach Reno inside an hour. You could call out until you get cell phone reception, talk to Carling and Rune and tell them what is going on while I go talk to this Malphas and see what I can do here."*

"I'm not leaving," she told him.

He looked as disturbed as she had ever seen him, and even a little angry. *"I don't want you to stay here."*

He was that worried about her?

She said gently, *"Duncan, think for a moment. It would be nice if one of us could leave and tell the outside world what is going on, but there is a Djinn involved, and information works both ways. What if Wendell decides that other people would be willing to pay for what he learned about us? What if one of them is the Djinn? Nobody here has any legal authority or any right to execute Vetta. Hanging her is* murder. *I could get halfway to Reno— hell, we could both leave and he could still stop us if he wanted to."* She paused to let that point sink in. *"We couldn't know it at the time, but we hit the point of no return the moment we stepped into Wendell's shop. We need to confront whatever this is together, head on. Right now."*

"Gods damn it," he whispered. His lips pulled back from his teeth where, she saw, a hint of his fangs showed. Then his grip on her elbows loosened, and he stroked his fingers lightly down her forearms before he let her go. "All right. Let's find Gehenna."

THE CASINO WAS easy to locate. It sat at the edge of the settlement in a large circus-sized tent. Raucous noise poured out of it, and drunks milled about the opening. Inside a blaze of electric lights flashed atop rows of slot machines. Malphas, or his casino managers, had invested in importing electric generators. Cigarette, cigar and hashish smoke hazed the air.

Seremela caught sight of movement out of the periphery of her vision and looked up. A boardwalk had been constructed around the edge of the tent where several large Goblins, weapons prominently displayed, walked and watched the crowd below.

Her lip curled. She and Duncan exchanged a glance then moved further into the tent where they found the game tables. People caught sight of Seremela and moved to give them both a wide berth.

She was okay with that. She wanted a three foot space between her and anyone else in this hellhole.

Male and female servers, both Elder Races and human, carried drinks and trays of chips for people to buy, dressed only in waist chains and dog collars. While Seremela wasn't a prude by any means, she didn't like strangers' dangly bits paraded in front of her without warning, and she jerked her gaze away with a muttered curse.

A human server approached them with a bright smile, although Seremela noted that he came up on Duncan's far side, staying well away from her. "Want to buy some chips?"

"We want a manager," Duncan said.

His smile never faltering, the server said, "Yeah, good luck with that. It's a busy night, but they're all real busy. Days too. Gehenna never closes, no matter how hot it gets. Offices are straight ahead."

"Thanks," Duncan said.

They barely took three steps forward when a female Vampyre, flanked by two Goblins, shouldered through the crowd toward them. The Vampyre had short blonde hair and was dressed in black fatigue pants and a black tank top, which showed off her muscled torso. She wore a semiautomatic in a hip holster and she moved like a fighter. She also looked intelligent, and she stopped right in front of them.

After one comprehensive glance at Duncan, the Vampyre focused on Seremela. "If you want to stay in Gehenna, you have to wrap up your snakes. You're disturbing the customers."

"We're not here to gamble and we have no intention of staying on the floor," Seremela said quietly. "We're here to talk to Malphas."

The Vampyre rubbed the back of her neck and studied them both under leveled brows. "You're here about the girl, aren't you?" she said. When neither of them confirmed nor denied, she shook her head. "Follow me."

Dismissing the two Goblins, the Vampyre led them through the crowd to the back of the tent. Then, without stopping, she led them outside through another opening. Behind the tent several modular buildings had been set up, the area surrounded by a nine foot high barbed wire fence. Seremela looked around everywhere as they walked. She knew in her bones that Vetta was very close, probably in one of these buildings.

"She's here," Seremela said to Duncan. *"I know she is."*

He moved as calmly as ever, hands loose at his sides, but she noticed how his sharp gaze roamed over the scene. *"I believe you,"* he said. *"I think she's here too."*

Their Vampyre escort was apparently not much for idle chitchat, for she didn't say a word until they reached the last modular building. Once there, she propped open the door and flipped on an inside light. Duncan looked in but didn't step inside. Seremela glanced in too. The interior was totally empty and lit by a single naked light bulb.

The Vampyre said, "If you want to talk to Malphas, go in and call him. He'll come or not, as it suits him. If you've changed your mind, leave. Either way, the hanging is at dawn."

Seremela clenched her fists and started after the Vampyre, snakes hissing. She ran into a barrier as Duncan's arm shot out to block her way. "Easy, darling," he said quietly to her. Telepathically, he said, *Don't waste your energy on her. She doesn't matter. We've got more important things to focus on.*

She sucked in a breath and struggled to rein in her temper. He was right. This Vampyre didn't matter in the slightest. She gave him a curt nod, and he dropped his arm and stepped inside. With one last glare at the Vampyre, Seremela followed.

Inside the building was just as bare and unadorned as her first glance had told her it was. Metal walls, metal floor, metal ceiling. No chairs, no carpet, no wall hangings or desks.

After they had both turned in a circle, Duncan shrugged at her and said into the apparent emptiness, "Malphas."

At first nothing happened, and a raging despair threatened to take Seremela over. He had to come. He had to.

Then black smoke slid into the building through the open door, and the air began to compress. Power built and built. It pressed against them so that Seremela's breathing felt constricted and she had to swallow hard. This was a very old one, possibly a first generation Djinn. What was a first generation Djinn doing at Devil's Gate?

The Power coalesced into the form of a tall, golden haired man, with an angelically beautiful face and two supernovas for eyes. Those piercing twin stars fixed on them, and the beautiful man gave them a deadly smile.

Malphas said, "Welcome to Gehenna."

Chapter Six

Love

"WHAT CAN I do for you?" the Djinn asked.

Danger breathed along the back of Duncan's neck. After one glance at him, Malphas turned to Seremela, who regarded him with a calm yet tense expression. Her snakes draped across her arms and shoulders, and all of them watched the Djinn too.

"We were told my niece is going to be executed for murder at dawn," Seremela said. "It isn't true. Vetta would not commit murder."

"Ah," said Malphas as he gestured with one long white hand. "I'm afraid that the truth has limited efficacy, especially here."

With that one simple sentence, the danger in the room skyrocketed.

No honorable Djinn that Duncan had ever met or heard of would have said such a thing, because the Djinn prized truth along with all other forms of information.

"Be careful," Duncan said to Seremela. She gave him a startled glance as he asked, "Which House are you with,

Malphas?"

The Djinn considered him for a moment. Then Malphas chuckled. "You believe the answer to this has any relevance?"

"With the Djinn," Duncan said in a polite tone of voice, "the answer to this is always relevant."

Malphas inclined his head in acknowledgment. "I hail from the House Shaytan."

"Currently?" Duncan asked.

Malphas's smile widened. "No."

"Duncan, what's going on?" Seremela's telepathic voice sounded tense.

He kept his attention fixed on the deadly creature in front of him, the muscles in his body clenching tight. *"He's a pariah, Seremela. A very Powerful one."*

"I don't know much about Djinn society," she said. Her expression turned fearful as she picked up on his wariness. *"I don't know what that means."*

"I do," he told her grimly.

The five Djinn Houses were built on their associations, and their associations were built on their word. A Djinn who broke his word was perceived as having no honor by other Djinn, and he became a pariah, without association with any of the Houses, lawless and rogue.

Seremela had said they had hit the point of no return when they stepped into Wendell's shop, but here at Gehenna they had stepped into a place that was far worse, and infinitely more dangerous.

Scary dude, Wendell had said about the Djinn. *I'm not sure what he cares about.*

A stiletto of cold, icy certainty sliced through Duncan.

Whatever Malphas cared about, it wasn't the truth, or the law. As a first generation Djinn, he would have the Power to know whether or not Vetta was telling the truth if she claimed she was innocent. Since he was still holding her in custody, he didn't care who had actually killed Thruvial. Hanging Vetta must benefit him in some way, only now Duncan and Seremela had shown up to protest.

Malphas hadn't come to this empty trailer to talk with them. He had come to figure out whether or not he should kill them too. The only reason why Duncan and Seremela were still alive was because the Djinn had not yet decided what course of action was in his best interest.

"Things were different when the girl was a nobody, weren't they?" Duncan said. Malphas strolled leisurely around him, and he turned to keep the Djinn in front of him. "Because then nobody cared if she died. What I don't understand is why hang her in the first place?"

"She's a stupid child," Malphas said. His tone was casually dismissive, as if they talked about a disobedient dog. "She's insolent and rude, and she has behaved as though everybody else owes her something. Before you arrived, there was no one here in Devil's Gate to miss her and several people who would say good riddance. In the meantime someone of Power—someone who had taken hold of a great deal of power here—has been killed, and there are many other Powerful creatures present who are disturbed by that. They want retribution. They want to know that the same thing cannot happen to them and go unpunished. They hear the word 'poison,' they see a medusa—" The Djinn let the sentence trail away as he shrugged. "The clamor to hang her became too loud to ignore. She had to be held somewhere, so I took her."

"Then give us a chance to find out who really killed him," Seremela said. Her eyes burned with repressed emotion but, Duncan was glad to see, her face and voice remained calm. "I'm—I've been a medical examiner. If I could examine the body, I can determine what type of poison was used and possibly learn a great deal more. I can guarantee you this much—even if Vetta's snakes bit him repeatedly, they're much too immature to carry enough poison to kill a mature Dark Fae male."

"Keep a poisoned, rotting corpse here, in this heat?" said Malphas, his beautiful face twisting with distaste. "Oh no, Doctor. While your offer might carry a certain theoretical merit, there is no body left for you to examine."

"What do you mean, there's no body?" Seremela asked tightly. "What happened to it?"

"Thruvial's own attendants lacked the proper Dark Fae herbs for preserving the dead. His remains turned so foul they were forced to burn him on a pyre yesterday."

As Duncan listened, his mind raced. Discovering

what the Djinn cared about was the key that would get them out of this trailer alive.

The Djinn didn't care who killed Thruvial, and he didn't especially care one way or another about using Vetta for a scapegoat, or he would have hanged her when Thruvial's murder had first been discovered.

Why had the Djinn gotten involved in the first place? What did he gain from it?

Then Duncan had it, what Malphas cared about.

Earlier Wendell the pharmacist had even coined the term. Malphas owed his life to balancing power. As a first generation Djinn who was also a pariah, he lived with the constant risk of being hunted by others of his kind.

For the other Djinn, however, killing Malphas would be exceedingly difficult and costly. They would be reluctant to do so unless they were given no other choice.

When the others in Devil's Gate had demanded action, Malphas had taken Vetta into custody and held off her execution for a few days, not because of a sense of justice, but because of a sense of self preservation.

All of that told Duncan a few things. The first was that Malphas did not expect to suffer any repercussions from Thruvial's death because he hadn't been involved.

However, Malphas would be involved in Vetta's death if they hanged her. He had to be sure that death wouldn't matter to anyone.

Duncan said, "This is the line you do not want to

cross, Malphas."

The Djinn turned those supernova eyes back onto Duncan. "You have my attention, Vampyre. Explain what you mean."

"You may not belong to a particular House, but we do. Our House cares what happens to us, they know where we are and their associations are strong," Duncan said. "Carling Severan is my maker, and while she no longer sits on the Elder tribunal, she still maintains connections and alliances with the most Powerful of the Djinn. Those connections include the head of the tribunal itself, Soren, and Soren's son, Khalil of the House Marid. In fact you may have heard, once Carling and Khalil went to war together against a first generation pariah Djinn. They won."

"I see," said Malphas. His eyelids dropped over the blazing stars of his eyes, shuttering his expression.

Duncan told the Djinn, "Whatever happened to Thruvial is none of our concern. We are not here to solve a murder, to get involved or to placate the locals, no matter how much a sense of separateness or entitlement they seem to have acquired here at Devil's Gate. We don't have to justify taking an innocent girl away from a dangerous situation. You will not stop us from retrieving her, nor will you harm us in any way as we leave, because if you do, you would bring that kind of war down on yourself, and really, Malphas, when it comes right down to it, none of us are worth that to you."

As Duncan talked, a quick patter of footsteps sounded outside. The Vampyre guard appeared in the open doorway, carrying a backpack on one shoulder while she held onto the arm of a young medusa with a tear-streaked face.

The medusa screamed, "Aunt Serrie!"

"Let go of my niece," Seremela said. The Vampyre tossed the backpack to the floor and let go of Vetta who flung herself forward. Seremela snatched her close.

"You are quite right," said the pariah Djinn with an angelic smile. "None of you are worth that."

SEREMELA CLENCHED THE GIRL so hard the muscles in her arms jumped, while Vetta buried her face into her neck and sobbed. Seremela watched as the Djinn dissolved into black smoke that dissipated into nothing. Duncan pivoted on his heel toward her, his lean face composed but his eyes glittered with a dangerous light.

She said fiercely, "We're done here, right?"

"We're done," he said. He sounded as calm as he always did, his rich voice mellow and soothing, but as he strode toward her he pulled his gun.

She sucked air, held Vetta tighter and said between her teeth, "What now?"

Sympathy darkened Duncan's gaze as he reached her side. He gripped her shoulder and said, "Malphas has chosen to disengage, but that doesn't mean anybody else at Devil's Gate has."

"Shit," she muttered. Of course he was right. She

looked around but the other Vampyre had disappeared as well.

Vetta lifted her head. Her eyes were smudged with streaks of black eyeliner, and her small, slender snakes were entirely subdued, curled quietly against her head. Seremela could see in her niece's young, exhausted face the ghost of the five-year-old Vetta had once been.

"I really need to go home now, Aunt Serrie," she whispered.

"Of course you do," she said gently. Now was not the time for recriminations or lectures. "Are you hurt?"

Vetta wiped at her face. "Just tired and hungry."

"All right." Seremela looked at the backpack that the Vampyre had tossed to the floor. "Is this yours?"

Vetta nodded. Duncan said, "We're not going to try to retrieve anything else. We're going straight to our car and leaving."

"That's fine, I don't care," said the girl, her voice wobbling. "I just want to get the hell out of here."

As Seremela turned her attention fully onto the backpack that Malphas's guard had tossed onto the floor, she immediately sensed a warm glow of aged Power. She bent and reached for the pack, scanning it carefully.

When she had been a medical examiner, most of the deaths she had autopsied had occurred through magical or Powerful means, and her magical sense was finely honed.

She was used to handling dangerous residual Power. Usually when she scanned for magic, she could compartmentalize it within moments. A spell cast by a human witch, an item infused with Dark Fae Power, Demonkind, Elven, Djinn or Light Fae—she knew the flavors and characteristics of all their magics, and most of the time she could either disable or contain the spells.

This, though. This was something different from anything she had ever encountered. The harder she concentrated, the deeper the well of Power felt underneath the veneer of that mild, mellow glow. For a moment she felt as though she might fall into something vaster than she had ever experienced.

Astonished and more than a little frightened, she jerked back and heard herself say sharply, "What do you have in there?"

"The goddamn Tarot deck from hell," Vetta said on a fresh sob.

She turned to stare at the girl. "Where on earth did you get something like that?"

Vetta's face twisted with a flash of her old rebellious self that crumpled quickly. She wailed, "I stole it a couple months ago. I'm already so, so sorry I ever set eyes on it, so I don't need for you to yell at me about it right now, all right?"

Seremela angled her jaw out. She said in a soft, even tone of voice, "I can't help but notice your choice of words, Vetta. You're sorry you set eyes on it, but you're not sorry you stole it?"

The girl's reddened eyes widened with fresh dismay.

Duncan said quietly, "This conversation can wait

until later. Seremela, is the pack too dangerous to take with us?"

She gave him a quick glance then turned her attention back to the pack. After a moment, she said, "It doesn't feel active at the moment, so I don't think so. It's a very old item of Power, though. We shouldn't just leave it."

"Then we'll take it," he said. "As long as you're willing to look after it and we leave right now."

She nodded, took the pack and slung it over one shoulder. Duncan strode to the trailer's open door and looked out. Moonlight edged his set expression and sharp gaze.

Seremela had grown accustomed reading to the subtle changes in his face. When she saw the line of his mouth harden, she asked, "What is it?"

"The only way out of this fenced-in enclosure is through the casino," he told her. "I noticed when we came in."

As soon as he mentioned it, she remembered the unbroken line of fence too.

She said to Vetta, "You keep your head down. You stick to me like glue, young lady, and above all, you keep quiet. I don't care if you see someone you don't like, or if someone says something you don't like. You do not antagonize anyone. Do you hear me?"

The girl bent her head and nodded, and Duncan led the way through the enclosure to the back of the casino, where bright flashes of color spilled out from the opening. It looked, Seremela thought uneasily, like the tent had been sliced open and was bleeding light.

They walked inside and along the main aisle.

Silence began to spread through the crowd. Seremela's stomach tightened as people stared at them. Then the whispering began. Vetta did as she had promised and kept her head down as she walked as close as she could get to Seremela without actually climbing on top of her.

Seremela put an arm around her niece's shoulders and several of her snakes wrapped around Vetta too. She tried as best as she could to adopt something of Duncan's calm, non-confrontational manner, while each step she took, each moment that passed, felt as though it took an hour. In vast contrast to how she had felt when they had come into the place, she glanced up at the armed Goblins on the walk overhead and felt grateful for their presence.

A ripple of reaction moved through the crowd like a wave, and she knew they weren't going to make it out of the casino without some kind of confrontation.

Duncan twisted to face the reaction. He still looked as prosaic as if he were taking out the trash, while her heart was jumping about in her chest like a cat on a hot tin roof. When she saw his lean, mildly interested profile, she felt a rush of emotion so powerful, it almost knocked her on her ass.

I love you, she thought. You have gone so far out of your way for me that you've traveled across the country.

You've faced down petty criminals and a rogue Djinn. You accepted without question when I said that Vetta was innocent, and you've done all of it with humor and kindness, and you're willing to do even this for my niece, whom you haven't even been properly introduced to.

How could I not love you?

How could I not?

The crowd parted and a Dark Fae woman approached. She was tall and slim, with the trademark angular features and overlarge gray eyes of the Dark Fae. Her gleaming black hair was pulled back in a braid, and she wore simple dark leggings and a sleeveless tunic.

She also wore a sword that remained in its harness, strapped to her back. Her hands were empty and lax at her sides as she came face to face with them.

Vetta broke her promise of silence in a whisper. "Xanthe."

Seremela's arm tightened on her in warning.

Other than a slight smile and crinkling of her eyes, an expression that was gone almost before Seremela had registered it, the Dark Fae woman gave no sign that she heard Vetta. Instead she turned to Duncan and said, "Please allow me to assist in escorting you safely from this place."

"Why should we?" Duncan asked.

"Because I, too, know that the girl is innocent," said the Dark Fae. She spoke English perfectly, with a trace of accent, and raised her voice as she said it, causing another reaction to ripple through the avid-looking onlookers.

"Then by all means," said Duncan, as he gestured to the aisle in front of him. "After you."

The woman Vetta had called Xanthe inclined her head and took the lead, while Duncan fell back. He gestured for Seremela and Vetta to go ahead of him, and he came up close behind them.

Warily, Seremela followed the Dark Fae woman, while she tried to think how the maneuver might possibly be a trap, but she couldn't see how—the woman had, after all, made very public declaration of Vetta's innocence and support.

They worked their way through the rest of the casino. With the Dark Fae ahead of them, and Duncan guarding them from behind, Seremela felt marginally more secure. She devoutly hoped it wasn't an illusion.

She asked Vetta telepathically, *"Do you know this woman?"*

"Not really," the girl said. *"I know who she is—or was, anyway. She was one of Thruvial's attendants. He had three. I guess that's traditional?"*

Vetta was correct. Dark Fae triads were quite traditional and appeared in various forms in their society. Seremela wondered where Thruvial's other two attendants were.

She said, *"Yes, it is. What do you know about her?"*

Vetta shrugged. She looked and sounded exhausted. *"Like I said, nothing much. She's quiet and keeps to herself."*

"Okay," Seremela said.

They fell silent. Later Seremela would have dreams about that hellish walk through Gehenna, the dreams filled with a creeping sense of dread while a host of creatures stared at her with hungry gazes and stalked close behind her, moving in for a kill.

Then finally they stepped out of the tent. The cooler desert night air outside was indescribably wonderful. Seremela and Vetta took deep breaths, almost staggering with relief, as the Dark Fae woman paused to look over her shoulder at them.

"Don't stop," murmured Duncan. "We need to go quickly."

Seremela nodded, and their small group moved into a different formation. This time the Dark Fae woman fell back to walk at Seremela's side, while Duncan moved up beside Vetta on the other side.

The Dark Fae woman said, "We should not go through the crowded part toward the center of the camp. It is quieter along the outskirts."

Duncan and Seremela looked at Vetta for confirmation. The girl said, "Xanthe's right. The camp's quieter around the edges."

"Show us," Duncan said.

Both Vetta and the Dark Fae woman did, and they were able to move quickly through the quiet, shadowed area. They had circumvented the encampment and reached the edge of the massive parking lot when Seremela couldn't keep quiet any longer.

She stopped, pulling Vetta to a halt. The other two

stopped as well.

Seremela said to the Dark Fae woman, "You. What is your name?"

"Xanthe Tenanye," replied the Dark Fae.

"You just left her there," Seremela said. "You knew Vetta was innocent, and you let them imprison her for—what, two days? She was terrified and all alone."

"I did not leave her," said Xanthe. Her large gray eyes seemed to gather all the meager illumination from the moonlight, while her hands remained at her sides. "I stayed in Gehenna for the last two days, watching while I tried to figure out what I could do for her. I would not have let them hang her."

"Interesting," said Duncan. He had moved so that he was much closer to the Dark Fae. "How did you know Vetta was innocent, and how would you have stopped it?"

"By confessing, if I had no other choice," said Xanthe Tenanye. "I knew Vetta didn't kill Cieran Thruvial, because I did."

"You're a killer?" Vetta said it with such a squeak of surprise it would have sounded comical in almost any other situation.

"You may call me such, if you must," said Xanthe.

"What are you still doing here?" Vetta asked. "They will hang you, if they realize you did it."

"I am well aware of that, but I was not free to leave until you were," said Xanthe. She looked around. "It is not safe to stay here and have this conversation. You still need to leave immediately."

Seremela and Duncan looked at each other. He murmured, "Understanding what happened or getting involved is still not our mission."

"My thoughts exactly," Seremela said grimly. She remembered where they had parked the SUV and started hauling Vetta in that direction.

That was when Vetta chose to dig in her heels, literally. By simply not moving, she dragged Seremela to a stop. "Why?" Vetta said raggedly to Xanthe. "They held me in a metal building without food or water, and I knew I was going to die. All of that was because you murdered someone, and I need to know why."

For the first time since she had approached them, Xanthe exposed emotion in her body language as she shifted sharply and rubbed the back of her neck. Then she said abruptly, "I work for the Dark Fae Queen. More accurately, I work for her chief of security. I didn't just murder Thruvial, I executed him on orders for crimes committed against the crown. I had no idea that you would get blamed for his death. Now will you go?"

As soon as the Dark Fae woman mentioned the Queen, Seremela and Duncan jerked to a halt. They stared at Xanthe.

"Oh hell," said Duncan. "She's telling the truth."

Seremela was beginning to feel dizzy from all the shifts in reality over the last few hours.

Murder. Illegal drugs. A pariah, and now inter-demesne politics. Oh, and she couldn't forget to add theft of a major item of Power to that list, not when its subtle, fathomless Power was slowly but surely soaking into the bones of her shoulder. It felt good, nourishing and exotic at the same time, and she didn't trust that feeling one iota.

Vetta had started to speak. Seremela interrupted her. "No more discussion." She had never used such a harsh tone of voice with her niece before. Vetta looked shocked and her mouth shut with a snap. Seremela steered her niece back around in the direction of their SUV as she said to Xanthe, "Thank you for watching out for my niece. Either come with us now or stay, and goodbye."

Duncan moved to Seremela's side with smooth, liquid grace. Xanthe took a few steps backward as she said, "My thanks, but you would be much safer withou—"

A new voice interrupted her. "We could not believe it, Xanthe, when we heard that you defended our lord's murderer and escorted her from Gehenna. Now we see your betrayal with our very own eyes."

For the second time that night, Duncan blurred. By the time Seremela had spun around, he already faced the two newcomers with his gun aimed at their heads.

They were Dark Fae, a male and a female, dressed like Xanthe in simple leggings and sleeveless tunics, with swords strapped to their backs. They stared from Xanthe to Vetta and Seremela, their expressions bitter with hate.

"She is innocent," said Xanthe as she drew her sword. "They will pass from this place unharmed."

"She's poison," spat the male. "She made no secret of how she loathed our lord, and now she has brought another of her kind who is even more poisonous." He and his companion drew their swords as well, and the sound of the long scrape of metal ran down Seremela's spine.

"Do they not comprehend that you have a gun trained on them?" Seremela said incredulously in Duncan's head.

Xanthe lunged, the others stepped to meet her and the clash of steel rang out.

"I can't use it and they know it," said Duncan. *"The gunshot would draw too much attention. The sound of the swordfight is bad enough."*

He tossed the gun at her. Shocked, she made an incoherent noise and let go of Vetta to stumble forward, just barely managing to catch it.

"I hope you can shoot," Duncan told her. "Use it as a last resort."

She stared at him, caught the moonlit edge of his shadowed smile, and then he sprang at the three fighting Dark Fae.

Vetta was whispering, "Oh gods, I just want to wake up and be in my own bed."

Seremela's hands shook as she checked the 9 mm. Duncan had put it on safety before he tossed it to her. She clicked it off and stood ready as she watched the fight. While she was by no means an expert, yes, she knew how to shoot.

"Get behind me," she told Vetta. The girl obeyed

and huddled shivering against her back. All of Seremela's snakes focused on the danger in front of her. Every muscle in her body was pulled as taut as piano wire, and she felt slightly nauseous as she tried to make sense of the melee.

They were so fast, all four of them, faster than she could track, and the Dark Fae were so difficult to tell apart in the silvery shadows. One struck another—oh, it was a bad blow—and that one grunted and went down on both knees, while Duncan engaged the third in a vicious flurry of blows and countermoves, and the fight was horribly, sickeningly unfair because his opponent had a sword while all he had was his knife.

A tic started at her temple, fluttering at a frenetic pace, because it was one thing to know how to shoot but quite another to know who to shoot, and just how was she supposed to tell when the last resort was, anyway? She pushed the heel of one hand against her temple as she tracked Duncan's opponent with the gun.

Duncan leaped forward, a fast, vicious attack. His opponent fell back and kept falling until he lay prone on the ground. It took a couple of heartbeats for Seremela to comprehend what had happened, because the violence ended as quickly and abruptly as it had started.

Two of the Dark Fae were down. Duncan and the third faced each other but didn't leap to attack each other. Seremela only recognized Xanthe for certain as the other woman reached over her head to sheathe her sword.

She lowered the gun, slid the safety back on and strode rapidly over to Duncan to fling her arms around him. He clenched her to him, one hand at the back of her neck.

"You're not hurt?" she whispered.

"No," he whispered back. "I'm all right."

Oh gods, thank you. She held onto him with all of her strength.

His lean cheek was cool against hers, the length of his body hard. He said, "Let's go home now."

She nodded. She couldn't trust herself to speak. In that moment, she thought those were the four most wonderful words in the English language.

Let's go home now.

Chapter Seven

Hearth

AFTER A NERVE wracking yet uneventful drive back to the Reno airport, they were airborne a couple of hours later and headed to Chicago where they would stop just long enough to allow Xanthe to disembark before they flew to Miami.

During the car trip Vetta drank three bottles of water, ate a couple of protein bars and had a crying jag against Seremela's shoulder as relief set in. As soon as they had cell phone reception, they called Seremela's sister, Camilla, and Vetta cried some more at her mother. Once they boarded the jet and took off, the girl disappeared into the lavatory for a while to emerge some time later, looking pale and exhausted but somewhat cleaner.

After Vetta finished, they all took turns washing up. Seremela sighed with relief as she rinsed the desert dust off her face, arms and neck.

Dawn spilled over the horizon. After shuttering all of the windows to block out the morning sun, the co-pilot served Xanthe, Vetta and Seremela bistro-style breakfast trays with fresh fruit, rolls, cheese, hard boiled eggs and smoked salmon, hot coffee and cream and fresh squeezed orange juice.

Duncan accepted a glass of bloodwine. Seremela frowned. After a sleepless, stressful night she was starving. He must be too. While bloodwine might do in a pinch, it did not have nearly the same nutritive qualities as fresh blood did.

Somewhat haltingly, she asked him, *"Will bloodwine be—sufficient for you, for now? I would be honored to help if you need fresh blood."*

Duncan smiled at her. He looked inexplicably sweet and roguish, and she thought he even looked somewhat embarrassed. Although she wasn't sure what prompted his expression, she could not help but smile back.

"That is very kind of you," he said. *"Bloodwine will be sufficient for now, thank you."*

She felt her cheeks warm and her gaze slid away from his. She had never fed a Vampyre directly from her vein before. Their bites were famous for inducing a sense of euphoria in their donors. Perhaps that was why he looked embarrassed. She glanced at Xanthe and Vetta. It was probably just as well he didn't need fresh blood at the moment.

Even though tiredness threatened to take her over, she ate quickly and drank several cups of coffee, fueled by a sense of purpose. She was not going to relax while they carried an unexamined item of Power on the plane.

As she ate, she listened to Duncan and Xanthe talk. Duncan asked, "Why kill Thruvial instead of taking him back to face trial?"

"He was the last nobleman involved in the conspiracy that killed the Queen's family," Xanthe said. "The problem with putting him on trial was that the evidence we managed to gather might not have been enough to convict him. Lord Black Eagle made the decision on the kill order."

The unfamiliar name caused Seremela to pause, until she realized that Xanthe referred to Tiago, the Wyr warlord who had mated with Niniane. She had met Tiago when she had been a medical examiner in Chicago, and she shuddered as she recalled Tiago's edgy demeanor. He had terrified her—she had no problem whatsoever imagining him taking responsibility for ordering someone's execution.

The Dark Fae woman was continuing. "It took me the better part of the year to work my way into Thruvial's household. He fled Adriyel as soon as the borders opened. The trials of his fellow conspirators had shaken him considerably, but it didn't stop him from committing other distasteful crimes at Devil's Gate—including sex trafficking, protection and blackmail."

"He was a horrible man," Vetta whispered, her head bent.

Seremela murmured gently, "Did he hurt you in any way?"

Vetta looked at her sidelong, and she could tell her

niece knew what she was really asking. Vetta shook her head and told her telepathically, *"He thought I was disgusting, but he wanted to put me out to customers who were interested in exotic experiences. The last time we talked—fought, actually—he threatened to scar my face if I didn't do as he said. I'm glad he's dead."*

Seremela breathed evenly, struggling to contain her rage as she listened. *"I'm glad he's dead too,"* she said.

She finished her breakfast, swallowed her last cup of coffee, set the breakfast tray aside and reached for Vetta's backpack. "Don't relax too much yet," she said to her niece who was drooping sideways in her seat. "You need to tell me about this Tarot deck from hell. Who did you steal it from?"

"I don't know," Vetta said. "She was just some woman at a rest stop. I lifted it from the back of her car when she went inside the gas station. I could tell it had a tingle of Power. At first I thought it was cool. Then every time I started to lay out a spread for myself, Death kept showing up. Every time, Aunt Serrie. It got so that I couldn't sleep. I kept checking the cards. Then I started to pray. I was so sure I was going to die." Her voice broke at the end.

Seremela touched the back of Vetta's hand in silent sympathy. Vetta watched miserably as Seremela searched through the pack, and Duncan and Xanthe grew quiet to watch too.

The pack didn't hold anything of much value. A couple packs of Marlboro Reds, a cigarette lighter, a scarf that smelled like patchouli and smoke, some cosmetics, a wallet with Vetta's I.D. and some cash. It was unusual that nobody had taken the cash or the Tarot cards themselves, but she suspected that employees who worked for Malphas were scrupulously careful about their conduct.

A wooden box lay at the bottom of the pack. She pulled it out and set it on the table. It was clearly the source of the glow of Power. The box's lid had a hand-painted, stylized face. One side of the face was male, the other side female. It was Taliesin, the god of the Dance.

She opened the box, pulled out the deck of cards and turned over the top one, a Major Arcana card. A picture of a golden woman, in a chariot with seven lions, smiled up at her. Inanna, the goddess of Love. She turned over a few of other cards, and each one was exquisite.

Aside from being an item of Power, the deck was a work of art. *Oh, Vetta.* She sighed and rubbed her forehead while she studied the deck.

Her initial impression remained the same. Underneath the veneer of quiet Power, the cards held a subtle but remarkable depth. Finally she sat back and shook her head, her mouth tight.

"I have no idea whose magic created this," she said. "It's not Light or Dark Fae, Elven, Wyr, Demonkind, human—or anything else I've encountered. It's more Powerful than it looks on the surface, and I'm not even sure what the Power does. Perhaps it's just meant to be a tool for divination. I don't know." She met Duncan's gaze as she said, "I don't sense anything overtly offensive in the magic, but I don't like magic I don't understand, and I don't trust it."

Xanthe reached out to touch one of the cards, her gray eyes wide. She said, "I think they're beautiful."

As the tips of Xanthe's long fingers touched the card, Seremela felt the Power in the deck pull toward the other woman. She said sharply, "Do you feel that?"

All three of the others stared at her and shook their heads. Vetta sat as far back from the deck as she could get, her hands tucked under her arms. Duncan asked, "What did you feel?"

"It's tugging toward you, like it wants to go to you," Seremela said to Xanthe.

"Oh please take the deck with you," said Vetta passionately. "Please take it far, far away."

SEREMELA DIDN'T WANT to take responsibility for the Tarot deck, and Vetta refused to touch it. Xanthe was willing to take the Tarot deck to Adriyel, to see if she could discover any answers about its origins and its maker from Dark Fae elders, so in the end that was what they decided to do.

The Dark Fae woman disembarked at Chicago's O'Hare with quiet thanks. As soon as the plane was in the air again, Vetta sprawled on the couch and fell asleep as soon as she went horizontal.

Duncan and Seremela moved to the back of the plane so that they didn't disturb the sleeping girl. He settled in the seat beside Seremela. She looked exhausted, with dark shadows under her eyes, but her gaze was clear and bright. She whispered, "I cannot thank you enough, Duncan."

"Shh," he said, just as softly. "There's no need."

"There's every need," she said, her words quiet but forceful. Her mouth worked, and her expression was so beautiful, so intense, Duncan had to put his arms around her and kiss her.

Her mouth. It was like everything else about her, sensitive and lavish with softness yet etched with determination and character. He loved her mouth; he loved it and he kissed and kissed her, while she twined her arms around his neck and kissed him back. Roused by her gentle, heartfelt response, his sexual aggression was lying in wait, ready to pounce. He held it tightly in check. Now was not the time.

Reluctantly he pulled away, and laughter threatened to take him over as he realized all of her snakes had wrapped around him again. He smiled into her gorgeous eyes. "Why do you always look so surprised whenever I touch you?"

She glanced away as she lifted a shoulder. "Many people are disgusted by the thought of touching us, much like Thruvial was with Vetta."

"Thruvial was a pig," Duncan said. That jerked her attention back to him. He said deliberately into her wide gaze, "I think you are the most beautiful woman I've ever met, inside and out."

Wonder lightened her feminine features. "You do?"

"I do. I learned a lot about you in a day."

"It was a long day," she pointed out.

He laughed softly. "It was a very long day. You're intelligent and curious, insightful and adventurous, and you're generous and caring. Even though you're gentle to the bone, you know how to shoot a gun, and you're so brave, especially when you're frightened." His smile turned crooked. "I hope you don't mind that I'm falling in love with you."

There it was again, that look of hers, stricken with wonder and trembling at the threshold of delight. She breathed, "I don't mind in the slightest."

"That's all right then." Because he had tensed up as he waited for her response, he relaxed and pressed a kiss to her forehead. "Did you know that *Rigoletto* is playing this season?"

She nestled close with a sigh. "I love Verdi's operas."

"I'll get us tickets," he promised, resting his cheek against her temple.

They grew quiet, and after a while Duncan thought she fell asleep. He couldn't. He was too full of the fabulous sensation of her curvaceous, warm body pressed against his side. He closed his eyes and drifted quietly, letting his imagination have free rein.

He wanted to do things with her. He wanted to talk over morning newspapers, hold hands in a movie theater, walk along the beach on a full moonlit night. He wanted her to call him and interrupt him while he was at

DEVIL'S GATE ✧ 111

work. He wanted to watch her enjoy a good meal.

He wanted to suckle her to climax, and spear into her soft body until he climaxed. He wanted to fall asleep in her arms.

He wanted to bite her so fucking bad.

He was so absorbed in the dark red of sensual anticipation, she shocked him utterly when she whispered against his neck, "I love you too."

Gods.

He'd known emptiness in his life, and he knew how to be alone. He'd had taken lovers for a time and then they had parted, and he had watched his human friends and family die. He had never known anyone to fill him up so completely by saying four of the most beautiful words in any language.

I love you too.

No longer immersed in a dark red quiet, he discovered himself in a place of shining light.

SEREMELA'S SISTER, CAMILLA, flew in from Atlanta. She was waiting for them at the airport in Miami when they arrived that afternoon. Camilla and Vetta fell sobbing into each other's arms, and after a moment Camilla turned to Seremela and roped her into the embrace. Hands in his pockets, Duncan stood back to give the women a little space. He grinned at the look Seremela gave him as she succumbed to Camilla's clutching hug.

Then it was his turn. "Thank you," Camilla said as she gripped both his hands. "Thank you so much. I—I feel like there's more I should say, but I just don't have the words."

"We'll meet properly some other time," Duncan told Seremela's sister. "In the meantime, you are most welcome. Enjoy having your daughter back safe and sound."

Seremela told her sister, "Vetta will fill you in on everything. I'm too tired to talk."

Camilla said, "I'll call you tomorrow?"

"That's fine." Seremela staggered as Vetta threw her arms around her, hugging her fiercely. They stood for a moment in intense silence. Whatever they said to each other was telepathic, meant for each other alone, which Duncan thought was fitting.

After Camilla and Vetta left, a valet brought his car around while Seremela turned awkward and tried to explain how she could take a taxi home. Duncan listened patiently then said, "Don't be silly. Of course I will see you home."

She gave him a deer-in-the-headlights look. He was so amused and intrigued by it, he strode two steps forward until his chest brushed the tips of her delicious breasts and he growled into her upturned face, "We have unfinished business."

Her tremulous mouth formed two silent words. "We do?"

Falling in love was a beautiful feeling, as long as he fell with her. He grinned and bent his head until their lips touched. Then he said silently into her parted lips, *"We do."*

The drive to her home was completed in fiery silence. She couldn't sit still and fidgeted, and her snakes roamed restlessly around her.

He didn't want her to sit still. He wanted her to fidget and flutter about, while he stalked his prey to capture her finally, finally—against a door, cabinet, couch, wherever the hell, it didn't matter, any of the images his heated imagination supplied him were just fine, because he would capture her, it was just a matter of time. The red darkness took him over, and he held himself under savage control as he drove with immaculate care through the heavy Friday Miami traffic.

Fear and violence always touched a Vampyre's life somehow. He had never realized how he had grown used to it, until he faced that goddamn pariah Djinn and grew shocked at Seremela facing danger and violence. She was too good, too fine; she loved opera and classic movies, and she lived in a civilized, lawful world, and she should never, ever have to face such violence again.

Dimly he realized he was allowing himself to react to what had happened, and by letting go, he was no longer in control.

The atmosphere in the car had grown excruciatingly charged by the time he drove into the underground garage at her apartment building. He pulled into a parking space. The quiet purr of the car engine faded. Seremela started to say something, her words stumbling and awkward.

Staring straight ahead, he interrupted her. "Invite me in."

She took in a quick breath. It shook a little, and his cock hardened at the small telltale sign. He turned to her and discovered her staring at him with that wide eyed, wondering look. Three of her snakes peered sideways from behind her head, staring at him too.

Laughter spilled out of him as the sight broke his tension. He reached out to one of the snakes. It touched the tip of his finger with a light flicker of its tongue. He repeated unsteadily, "Invite me in, Seremela. Please."

"I would love for you to come in," she whispered all in a rush.

With that, he lost all capacity for words or coherent thought. Somehow they got out of the car and into the elevator, where he backed her into a corner. He planted one hand on the wall on either side of her head and stared into her eyes as he breathed in the scent of her arousal. Her breathing grew choppy, and he watched the muscles in her slender throat move as she swallowed, the iridescent pattern that marked her skin shimmering in the overhead light.

Her lovely, slender throat.

His fangs descended. His face twisted as he fought himself. This was too far out of control. He was a stranger to himself.

Her warm, trembling hands smoothed the material of his T-shirt across his chest. "It's all right," she whispered. "I want you to bite me."

He hadn't even been aware that he'd taken a useless breath of air until it rushed out of him. The force of his own reaction nearly sent him to his knees.

"Duncan," she said. She sounded and looked dazed.

He lowered his head slowly, and ran his mouth along the leaping pulse at her neck, tonguing the delectable delicate flesh.

She pushed him, startling him out of his preoccupation. With a husky, drunken laugh, she pointed behind him. He looked over his shoulder. The elevator doors stood open. Ah, right.

The length of the hallway to her front door was all but unendurable. He said hoarsely, "After we go to the opera, what are we doing next?"

"I don't know," she moaned. She dropped her keys and bent over to retrieve them. "How about a weekend in bed?"

He blurred, snatched the keys out from underneath her hand and unlocked and opened her door before she could fully react. "Get inside."

He glared as she exploded with laughter. Then he laughed too. This was crazy, ludicrous. He could say he hadn't felt this way since he was a teenager, except he was certain he hadn't felt this way then either.

Then finally they were inside, alone in her shadowed apartment. She tossed her purse onto the couch—he realized they had forgotten her case, in the trunk of his car—and then he lost that thought too as she leaped at him. He snatched her up as she wrapped her arms and legs around him, and he strode for the bedroom.

"Say it again," he said. "What you told me on the plane."

Her brilliantly colorful eyes were luminous with emotion and desire. "I didn't think you heard me."

He laid her on the bed gently and straightened. He tore off his shirt. "I heard you. Say it again."

She pushed up to kneel on the bed in front of him, and she met his gaze as she reached for the fastening of his jeans. "I love you, Duncan."

"That was even better than the last time," he whispered, smiling as he palmed her full, soft breast. She pulled his jeans open and slid her hands inside them as she eased the material down over his lean hips. An odd sensation slid along his torso and up his arms. He glanced down at her snakes as they journeyed across his skin.

Seremela followed the direction of his gaze and drew back a little, her expression turning self-conscious. She offered softly, "I can wrap them, if you'd rather."

He said firmly, "No."

She pulled a few snakes away from him. "Are you sure it isn't too—tentacley for you?"

He grasped her shoulders and looked deeply into her eyes. "Listen to me. I did not say I was falling in love with you, if only you would hide some part of yourself or change some aspect to try to please me. I said I was falling in love with you—all of you. I don't want you to curb yourself, deny yourself, cover up your face or head or any part of your body. I don't want you to lose or gain weight, or watch what you say, or deny how you feel, or try to be anything but who you are, because who you are is the most beautiful person in the world to me."

As she listened, the expression on her lovely features grew vulnerable, wide open. While he certainly hoped that he had not been the first person to ever tell her such things, he selfishly hoped that he had been the first male to do so. He grasped one of her snakes, kissed it on the nose and looked into its face. "You're never going to bite me, are you?"

"They would never hurt you," Seremela said. "They would die first."

"Oh well," he said, giving her a crooked grin. "There's goes that fantasy."

Her eyes went very wide, and she laughed, a joyous, surprised sound. She unbuttoned her top and shrugged out of it then slipped off her bra as Duncan kicked off his jeans and stood nude, his heavy erection jutting from his hips.

Her breasts were stunning, lush and full, the soft, plump nipples several shades darker than the light creamy green of her flesh. He bent, took one nipple in his mouth and sucked at it gently. The muffled noise that came out of her was urgent and incoherent. She cradled his head, ran her fingers through his hair and stroked his shoulders.

As he suckled her, a feather light sensation flickered along the sensitive skin on the head of his penis, creating a sharp, tantalizing pleasure. He looked down, as the sensation spread along the tight, drawn up sac of his testicles, and along the muscles of his lower abdomen.

Seremela's snakes flickered their slender tongues along his skin.

Seremela cocked her head and looked down as well. "They're tasting you," she said, giving him a sidelong smile. "They know that I love you, and they're curious." She looked splendid and barbaric, and completely unfettered.

For a moment, the ghost of the human Duncan once was struggled with the image. But Seremela's snakes were not mundane creatures; they were a part of her, and Duncan had not been human for a very long time.

His fangs descended. Seremela looked at his mouth and her gaze turned heavy lidded. She bared her neck to him in wordless invitation, and he gathered her soft, curvaceous body into his arms and eased his fangs gently into the pulse at her neck.

The moan that came out of her was full of sex and surrender, the sound shivering along his heated senses as hot blood spilled into his mouth, and it was so strange, so strange. He was twisted up inside, his desire for her out of control. He growled as he drank from her, while she arched against him, gasping. Her blood was stronger than human blood. It punched through him and made the world spin.

He lifted his head away from her, breathing raggedly, and only then realized she was struggling in his arms. For a terrible moment he felt sickened and disoriented—until he realized what she was trying to do.

"Help me get out of these damn jeans," she whimpered.

His fingers shook as he helped her to ease the jeans down to her knees. Then she lay back on bed and raised her legs so he could tug them off the rest of the way.

Wholly naked, she stretched, her eyes glazed with the lingering pleasure from his bite, and she looked beautiful and mysterious at once, all woman and wholly inhuman. He stroked his fingers up her inner thigh and fingered the velvet soft petals of her sex that were already wet with pleasure. She grasped his cock in one hand, stroking it as she parted her legs and told him, "Come inside now."

"I want to help you climax first," he whispered. He found her stiff little bud, so delicate and luscious, and he rolled the ball of his thumb over it.

She jerked uncontrollably and gasped. "It feels too good. It's too intense."

"That's partly from the bite," he crooned. "Everything's more intense right now." He slid two fingers into her, and she was softer and wetter than anything he had ever felt before, and so goddamn snug, he knew when he finally entered her, she was going to grip him tighter than a fist. He fucked her gently with his fingers while he continued to massage her clitoris.

"I can't take it," she sobbed. She gripped his wrist.

"You can take it," he told her. While he worked her,

he bent over to take her nipple in his mouth again, suckling at her carefully because his fangs were still descended and he did not want to scratch her. He was drowning in his own pleasure, drowning, immersed in her escalating pleasure as she undulated her hips.

Then she put a hand to the back of his head and pulled him down hard against her breast. His fangs broke the tender skin at her breast, and her Powerful blood filled his mouth again. Astonished, he sucked her hard while he drove his fingers into her, and she bucked underneath his hold and screamed as she climaxed.

He was blind with his own euphoria and still throbbing with need. He held himself rigidly, his palm pressed firmly against her clit while her inner muscles pulsed against his fingers. He would not draw out, not leave her until her climax was done, but then she shocked him again as she pulled his hand away. She rose and pushed him onto his back, and as he acquiesced, she came up over him and straddled him. She was the most amazing sight he had ever seen, her beautiful face stamped with intensity as she took his cock, positioned him and lowered herself down on him.

"Jesus," he said. His own climax shot like a bullet. He gripped her hips and bucked hard underneath her, swearing.

She collapsed on him, and he hugged her with his whole body. After a few minutes, she asked, "We're going to do this a lot, aren't we?"

"God, I hope so," he said.

They slept just like that, with him still inside of her and her sprawled like a rag doll on him.

He woke first. His erection had softened, and he didn't want to move and slip outside of her or wake her up. She was a soft, warm weight lying on him, and he loved it, loved it.

So he drifted a while and let his mind meander. Maybe she liked jewelry. Maybe she would enjoy a ring.

Maybe she would enjoy it especially if he went down on one knee to give it to her.

He had always thought he would enjoy marriage, and he believed he would make a good husband for the right woman. He had just never found the right woman, until now.

But he was getting way ahead of himself. They hadn't even gone on their first date yet. Speaking of which, he had opera tickets to buy.

Wait. He yawned and asked, "What day is it?"

"Nnh." Just when he was sure she had fallen back asleep, she murmured, "Think it's Friday?"

"Excellent. I think our first date should start right now."

She scratched her nose. "You don't have opera tickets yet."

"That's going to have to be our second date," he told her.

She opened her eyes and squinted at him. "What's our first date?"

He rolled her onto her back, reversing their

positions, and grinned down at her. "My vote is for that weekend in bed."

She snickered. "Ooh, that's my vote too. At some point we should call Carling and Rune and tell them we're back."

"We can do that Monday." He palmed her breast as his cock stiffened against her thigh. "We should also plan our third date soon."

"Mm, we should." Her gaze grew heavy lidded as she fingered his penis. "I'm so glad to be back in my own bed."

"I'm glad to be in your bed too." He moved his hips lazily, pushing against her hand.

Her expression softened with equal parts pleasure and affection. "So do you have any ideas about that third date?"

Duncan cocked his head, considering her. He thought about telling her about buying a ring, and him going down on one knee, but he didn't want to spook her. Instead he said, very casually, "I thought we might go shopping."

"You like to shop?" she asked in sleepy surprise.

"Yes, I do, sometimes. When I know I'm looking for something special." He bent to nuzzle her throat.

She made a purring sound and stroked his back. "It sounds like you've got something specific in mind for your shopping trip."

"Our shopping trip," he corrected.

"Okay, our shopping trip."

"And I do have something specific in mind, but for now, I think we should focus on our first date."

Giddy with happiness, he kissed her in a soft lingering caress. They lived in a crowded and dangerous world, but somehow she had become the only person in it. Right here and now, they were the only two people in the world, the only two.

"Duncan, do you by any chance play the piano?" she murmured.

He chuckled. "Why on earth would you ask me that?"

She stroked his face. "You just gave me a certain look."

Amused, he asked, "A look that said I play the piano?"

She tapped his nose with one finger. "Tell me you have a Bogart suit. Oh forget it, you have lots of suits, and they're all more beautiful than any of the clothes I own. Do you by any chance believe in precognition?"

He announced, "I am completely at sea in this conversation."

"Then we should probably stop talking," she whispered. She rolled her hips at him.

"I'm okay with that," he said.

He proceeded to make love to her again on their most excellent first date, and neither one said anything coherent for a long time.

Thank you!

Dear Readers,

Thank you for reading Devil's Gate! I hope you enjoyed reading about Duncan and Seremela.

Would you like to stay in touch and hear about new releases? You can:

- Sign up for my monthly email at: www.theaharrison.com
- Follow me on Twitter at @TheaHarrison
- Like my Facebook page at facebook.com/TheaHarrison

Reviews help other readers find the books they like to read. I appreciate each and every review, whether positive or negative.

Happy reading!
~*Thea*

Coming Soon:

Hunter's Season by Thea Harrison

As an assassin for the Dark Fae, Xanthe always wore a mask, hiding her emotions to do her duty. But when her identity is compromised, she trades undercover work for guarding Queen Niniane—a position that often brings her in contact with Chancellor Aubrey Riordan.

A year ago Aubrey's wife tried to assassinate their new queen in his name, a betrayal of everything he believes in. And now an attack on his life proves the dark conspiracy is not yet over. Although injured and weak, Aubrey can't help but be drawn to the shy assassin and loyal protector to the queen. Xanthe is everything Naida wasn't, and the passion she stirs in him is something he thought had long passed him by.

The Wicked by Thea Harrison

For a librarian with a focus on rare magical books, Olivia's new job is a dream come true. She's been hired as part of a team to help manage the safe transportation of the collection of books owned by the Vampyre sorceress Carling Severan. The fact that the library is located on a mysterious island in an Other land only heightens the adventure.

Head of security for the expedition, Sebastian Hale is tired of his rootless life of adventure and finds himself attracted to the calm, beautiful librarian. But he's living a personal nightmare. He's been hit with a curse that is slowly taking away his sight, and he doesn't know if he'll survive the results.

But the powerful feelings growing between them, along with Sebastian's inner turmoil, take a backseat when they learn there's a traitor in their expedition team. With Elder Races politics and a priceless library on the line, they'll have to rely on each other to survive.

Look for these titles from Thea Harrison

THE ELDER RACES SERIES – FULL LENGTH NOVELS

Published by Berkley

Dragon Bound

Storm's Heart

Serpent's Kiss

Oracle's Moon

Lord's Fall

Kinked

Night's Honor

Midnight's Kiss

Shadow's End

MOONSHADOW TRILOGY

Moonshadow

Spellbinder

Lionheart *Early 2018

ELDER RACES NOVELLAS

True Colors

Natural Evil

Devil's Gate

Hunter's Season

The Wicked

Dragos Takes a Holiday

Pia Saves the Day

Peanut Goes to School

Dragos Goes to Washington

Pia Does Hollywood
Liam Takes Manhattan

GAME OF SHADOWS SERIES
Published by Berkley

Rising Darkness
Falling Light

ROMANCES UNDER THE NAME
AMANDA CARPENTER

E-published by Samhain Publishing
(original publication by Harlequin Mills & Boon)
*These stories are currently out of print

A Deeper Dimension
The Wall
A Damaged Trust
The Great Escape
Flashback
Rage
Waking Up
Rose-Coloured Love
Reckless
The Gift of Happiness
Caprice
Passage of the Night
Cry Wolf
A Solitary Heart
The Winter King

Made in the USA
Middletown, DE
11 June 2024